POODLE SPRINGS

POODLE SPRINGS

Raymond Chandler
AND Robert B. Parker

BERKLEY BOOKS, NEW YORK

THE BERKLEY PUBLISHING GROUP
Published by the Penguin Group
Penguin Group (USA) Inc.
375 Hudson Street, New York, New York 10014, USA
Penguin Group (Canada), 90 Eglinton Avenue East, Suite 700, Toronto, Ontario M4P 2Y3, Canada
(a division of Pearson Penguin Canada Inc.)
Penguin Books Ltd., 80 Strand, London WC2R 0RL, England
Penguin Group Ireland, 25 St. Stephen's Green, Dublin 2, Ireland (a division of Penguin Books Ltd.)
Penguin Group (Australia), 250 Camberwell Road, Camberwell, Victoria 3124, Australia
(a division of Pearson Australia Group Pty. Ltd.)
Penguin Books India Pvt. Ltd., 11 Community Centre, Panchsheel Park, New Delhi—110 017, India
Penguin Group (NZ), 67 Apollo Drive, Rosedale, North Shore 0632, New Zealand
(a division of Pearson New Zealand Ltd.)
Penguin Books (South Africa) (Pty.) Ltd., 24 Sturdee Avenue, Rosebank, Johannesburg 2196,
South Africa

Penguin Books Ltd., Registered Offices: 80 Strand, London WC2R 0RL, England

This is a work of fiction. Names, characters, places, and incidents either are the product of the author's imagination or are used fictitiously, and any resemblance to actual persons, living or dead, business establishments, events, or locales is entirely coincidental. The publisher does not have any control over and does not assume any responsibility for author or third-party websites or their content.

PRINTING HISTORY
G. P. Putnam's Sons hardcover edition / October 1989
Berkley mass-market edition / November 1990
Berkley trade paperback edition / July 2010

Berkley trade paperback ISBN: 978-0-425-23934-6

The Library of Congress has cataloged the G. P. Putnam's Sons hardcover edition as follows:

Chandler, Raymond, 1888–1959.
  Poodle Springs/Raymond Chandler and Robert B. Parker.
    p. cm.
  "Based upon and incorporating the unfinished Raymond Chandler novel,
The Poodle Springs story"—T.p. verso.
I. Parker, Robert B., date.   II. Title.
ISBN 0-399-13482-4
PS3505.H3224P66   1989   89-10414 CIP
813'.52—dc20

PRINTED IN THE UNITED STATES OF AMERICA

10 9 8 7 6 5 4 3 2 1

As always, for Joan;
and this time, surely, for Cissy.
—R. P.

1

Linda stopped the Fleetwood convertible in front of the house without turning into the driveway. She leaned back and looked at the house and then looked at me.

"It's a new section of the Springs, darling. I rented the house for the season. It's a bit on the chi-chi side, but so is Poodle Springs."

"The pool is too small," I said. "And no springboard."

"I've permission from the owner to put one in. I hope you will like the house, darling. There are only two bedrooms, but the master bedroom has a Holly-wood bed that looks as big as a tennis court."

"That's nice. If we don't get on together, we can be distant."

"The bathroom is out of this world—out of any world. The adjoining dressing room has ankle-deep pink carpeting, wall to wall. It has every kind of cosmetic you ever heard of on three plate-glass shelves. The toilet—if you'll excuse my being earthy—is all alone in an annex with a door and the toilet cover has a large rose on it in *relief.* And every room in the house looks out on a patio or the pool."

"I can hardly wait to take three or four baths. And then go to bed."

"It's only eleven o'clock in the morning," she said demurely.

"I'll wait until eleven-thirty."

"Darling, at Acapulco—"

"Acapulco was fine. But we only had the cosmetics you brought with you and the bed was just a bed, not a pasture, and other people were allowed to dunk in the swimming pool and the bathroom didn't have any carpet at all."

"Darling, you *can* be a bastard. Let's go in. I'm paying twelve hundred dollars a month for this dive. I want you to like it."

"I'll love it. Twelve hundred a month is more than I make being a detective. It'll be the first time I've been kept. Can I wear a sarong and paint my little toenails?"

"Damn you, Marlowe, it's not my fault that I'm rich. And if I have the damn money I'm going to spend it. And if you are around some of it is bound to rub off on you. You'll just have to put up with that."

"Yes, darling." I kissed her. "I'll get a pet monkey and after a while you won't be able to tell us apart."

"You can't have a monkey in Poodle Springs. You have to have a poodle. I have a beauty coming. Black as coal and very talented. He's had piano lessons. Perhaps he can play the Hammond organ in the house."

"We got a Hammond organ? Now that's something I've always dreamed of doing without."

"Shut up! I'm beginning to think I should have married the Comte de Vaugirard. He was rather sweet, except that he used perfume."

"Can I take the poodle to work? I could have a small electric organ, one of the babies you can play if you have an ear like a corned beef sandwich. The poodle could play it while the clients lie to me. What's the poodle's name?"

"Inky."

"A big brain worked on that one."

"Don't be nasty or I won't—you know."

"Oh, yes you will. You can hardly wait."

She backed the Fleetwood and turned it into the driveway. "Never mind the garage door. Augustino will put the car away, but you don't really have to in this dry desert climate."

"Oh yeah, the house boy, butler, cook and comforter of sad hearts. Nice kid. I like him. But there's something wrong here. We can't get along on just one Fleetwood. I have to have one to drive to the office."

"Goddamn you! I'll get my white whip out if you're not polite. It has steel inserts in the lash."

"The typical American wife," I said and went around the car to help her out. She fell into my arms. She smelled divine. I kissed her again. A man turning off a sprinkler in front of the next house grinned and waved.

"That's Mister Tomlinson," she said between my teeth. "He's a broker."

"Broker, stoker, what do I care?" I went on kissing her.

We had been married just three weeks and four days.

2

It was a very handsome house except that it stank decorator. The front wall was plate glass with butterflies imprisoned in it. Linda said it came from Japan. The floor of the hall was carpeted with blue vinyl with a geometric design in gold. There was a den off of this. It contained plenty of furniture, also four enormous brass candle holders and the finest inlaid desk I had ever seen. Off the den was a guest bath, which Linda called a lavatory. A year and a half in Europe had taught her to speak English. The guest bath had a shower and a dressing table and a four-by-three mirror over it. The hi-fi system had speakers in every room. Augustino had turned it on softly. He appeared in the door, smiling and bowing. He was a nice-looking lad, part Hawaiian and part Japanese. Linda had picked him up when we made a short trip to Maui before going to Acapulco. It's wonderful what you can pick up if you have eight or ten million dollars.

There was an interior patio with a large palm tree and some tropical shrubs, and a number of rough stones picked up on the high desert for nothing, but $250 apiece to the customer. The bathroom which Linda had not overstated had a door to the patio and this had a door to the pool and to the interior patio and the outside patio. The living room carpet was pale grey, and the Hammond organ had been built out into a bar at the end opposite the keyboard. That nearly threw me. Also in the living room were couches matching the carpet and contrasting easy chairs and an enormous cowled indoor fireplace six feet away from the wall. There was a Chinese chest that looked very genuine and on the wall three embossed Chinese dragons. One wall was entirely of glass, the others of brick in colors to go with the carpet up to about five feet, and glass above that.

The bathroom had a sunken bath and sliding-door closets big enough to hold all the clothes twelve debutantes could want to buy.

Four people could have slept comfortably in the

Hollywood bed in the main bedroom. It had a pale blue carpet and you could read yourself to sleep by the light of lamps mounted on Japanese statuettes.

We went on to the guest room. It had matching single, not twin, beds, an adjoining bath with the same enormous mirror over the dressing table, and the same four or five hundred dollars' worth of cosmetics and perfumes and God knows what on the three plate-glass shelves.

That left the kitchen. It had a bar at its entrance, a wall closet with twenty kinds of cocktail, highball and wine glasses, beyond that a top-burner stove without an oven or broiler, two electric ovens and an electric broiler against another wall, also an enormous refrigerator and a deep freeze. The breakfast table had a pebbled glass top and wide comfortable chairs on three sides and a built-in couch on the fourth side. I turned on the cowl ventilator. It had a wide slow sweep that was almost silent.

"It's too rich for me," I said. "Let's get divorced."

"You dog! It's nothing to what we'll have when we build a house. There are things here that are a bit too gaudy but you can't say the house is bare."

"Where is the poodle going to sleep, in the guest bed or with us? And what color pajamas does he like?"

"Stop it!"

"I'm going to have to dust my office after this. I'd feel inferior if I didn't."

"You're not going to have any office, stupid. What do you suppose I married you for?"

"Come into the bedroom again."

"Blast you, we have to unpack."

"I bet Tino is doing it right now. There's a boy who looks like he could take hold. I must ask him if he minds my calling him Tino."

"Maybe he can unpack. But he won't know where I want my things. I'm fussy."

"Let's have a fight about the closets, who gets which. Then we could wrestle a bit, and then—"

"We could have a shower and a swim and an early lunch. I'm starving."

"You have an early lunch. I'll go downtown and look for an office. There must be some business in Poodle Springs. There's a lot of money here and I might grab off an occasional nickel."

"I hate you. I don't know why I married you. But you were so insistent."

I grabbed her and held her close. I browsed on her eyebrows and her lashes, which were long and tickly. I passed on to her nose and cheeks, and then her mouth. At first it was just a mouth, then it was a darting tongue,

then it was a long sigh, and two people as close as two
people can get.

"I settled a million dollars on you to do with as you
like," she whispered.

"A nice kind gesture. But you know I wouldn't touch
it."

"What are we to do, Phil?"

"We have to ride it out. It's not always going to be
easy. But I am not going to be Mr. Loring."

"I'll never change you, will I?"

"Do you really want to make a purring pussycat out
of me?"

"No. I didn't marry you because I had a lot of money
and you had hardly any. I married you because I love
you and one of the things I love you for is that you don't
give a damn for anybody—sometimes not even for me.
I don't want to make you cheap, darling. I just want to
try to make you happy."

"I want to make *you* happy. But I don't know how.
I'm not holding enough cards. I'm a poor man married
to a rich wife. I don't know how to behave. I'm only
sure of one thing—shabby office or not, that's where
I became what I am. That's where I will be what I will
be."

There was a slight murmur and Augustino appeared

in the open doorway bowing, with a deprecating smile on his elegant puss.

"At what time would Madame prefer luncheon?"

"May I call you Tino?" I asked him. "Only because it's easier."

"But certainly, sir."

"Thank you. And Mrs. Marlowe is not Madame. She is Mrs. Marlowe."

"I am very sorry, sir."

"Nothing to be sorry about. Some ladies like it. But my wife bears my name. She would like her lunch. I have to go out on business."

"Very good, sir. I'll prepare Mrs. Marlowe's lunch at once."

"Tino, there is one other thing. Mrs. Marlowe and I are in love. That shows itself in various ways. None of the ways are to be noticed by you."

"I know my position, sir."

"Your position is that you are helping us to live comfortably. We are grateful to you for that. Maybe more grateful than you know. Technically you are a servant. Actually you are a friend. There seems to be a protocol about these things. I have to respect protocol just as you do. But underneath we are just a couple of guys."

He smiled radiantly. "I think I shall be very happy here, Mr. Marlowe."

You couldn't say how or when he disappeared. He just wasn't there. Linda rolled over on her back and lifted her toes and stared at them.

"What do I say now! I wish the hell I knew. Do you like my toes?"

"They are the most adorable set of toes I have ever seen. And there seems to be a full set of them."

"Get away from me, you horror. My toes *are* adorable."

"May I borrow the Fleetwood for a little while? To-morrow I'll fly to L.A. and pick up my Olds."

"Darling, does it have to be this way? It seems so unnecessary."

"For me there isn't any other way," I said.

3

The Fleetwood purred me down to the office of a man named Thorson whose window said he was a realtor and practically everything else except a rabbit fancier.

He was a pleasant-looking baldheaded man who didn't seem to have a care in the world except to keep his pipe lit.

"Offices are hard to find, Mr. Marlowe. If you want one on Canyon Drive, as I assume you do, it will cost you."

"I don't want one on Canyon Drive. I want one on some side street or on Sioux Avenue. I couldn't afford one on the main stem."

I gave him my card and let him look at the photostat of my license.

"I don't know," he said doubtfully. "The police department may not be too happy. This is a resort town and the visitors have to be kept happy. If you handle divorce business, people are not going to like you too well."

"I don't handle divorce business and people very seldom like me at all. As for the cops, I'll explain myself to them, and if they want to run me out of town, my wife won't like it. She has just rented a pretty fancy place in the section out near Romanoff's new place."

He didn't fall out of his chair but he damn well had to steady himself. "You mean Harlan Potter's daughter? I heard she had married some—well the hell with it, what do I mean? You're the man, I take it. I'm sure we can fix you up, Mr. Marlowe. But why do you want it on a side street or on Sioux Avenue? Why not right in the best section?"

"I'm paying with my own money. I don't have a hell of a lot."

"But your wife—"

"Listen good, Thorson. The most I make is a couple of thousand a month—gross. Some months nothing at all. I can't afford a showy layout."

He lit his pipe for about the ninth time. Why the hell do they smoke them if they don't know how?

"Would your wife like that?"

"What my wife likes or dislikes doesn't enter into our business, Thorson. Have you got anything or haven't you? Don't con me. I've been worked on by the orchids of the trade. I can be had, but not by your line."

"Well—"

A brisk-looking young man pushed the door open and came in smiling. "I represent the *Poodle Springs Gazette*, Mr. Marlowe. I understand—"

"If you did, you wouldn't be here." I stood up. "Sorry, Mr. Thorson, you have too many buttons under your desk. I'll look elsewhere."

I pushed the reporter out of the way and goofed my way out of the open door. If anybody ever closes a door in Poodle Springs, it's a nervous reaction. On the way out I bumped into a big florid man who had four inches and thirty pounds on me.

"I'm Manny Lipshultz," he said. "You're Philip Marlowe. Let's talk."

"I got here about two hours ago," I said. "I'm looking for an office. I don't know anybody named Lipshultz. Would you please let me by?"

"I got something for you maybe. Things get known in this burg. Harlan Potter's son-in-law huh? That rings a lot of bells."

"Blow."

"Don't be like that. I'm in trouble. I need a good man."

"When I get an office, Mr. Lipshultz, come and see me. Right now I have deep affairs on my mind."

"I may not be alive that long," he said quietly. "Ever hear of the Agony Club? I own it."

I looked back into the office of Señor Thorson. The newshawk and he both had their ears out a foot.

"Not here," I said. "Call me after I talk to the law." I gave him the number.

He gave me a tired smile and moved out of the way. I went back to the Fleetwood and tooled it gracefully to the cop house down the line a little way. I parked in an official slot and went in. A very pretty blonde in a policewoman's uniform was at the desk.

"Damn all," I said. "I thought policewomen were hard-faced. You're a doll."

"We have all kinds," she said sedately. "You're Philip Marlowe, aren't you? I've seen your photo in the L.A. papers. What can we do for you, Mr. Marlowe?"

"I'm checking in. Do I talk to you or to the duty sergeant? And which street could I walk down without being called by name?"

She smiled. Her teeth were even and as white as the snow on top of the mountain behind the Springs. I bet she used one of the nineteen kinds of toothpaste that are better and newer and larger than all the others.

"You'd better talk to Sergeant Whitestone." She opened a swing gate and nodded me toward a closed door. I knocked and opened it and I was looking at a calm-looking man with red hair and the sort of eyes that every police sergeant gets in time. Eyes that have seen too much nastiness and heard too many liars.

"My name's Marlowe. I'm a private eye. I'm going to open up an office here if I can find one and if you let me." I dumped another card on the desk and opened my wallet to let him look at my license.

"Divorce?"

"Never touch it, Sergeant."

"Good. That helps. I can't say I'm enthusiastic, but we could get along, if you leave police business to the police."

"I'd like to, but I've never been able to find out just where to stop."

He scowled. Then he snapped his fingers. He yelled, "Norman!"

The pretty blonde opened the door. "Who is this character?" the sergeant wailed. "Don't tell me. Let me guess."

"I'm afraid so, Sergeant," she said demurely.

"Hell! It's bad enough to have a private eye mousing

around. But a private eye who's backed by a couple or three hundred million bucks—that's inhuman."

"I'm not backed by any two hundred million, Sergeant. I'm on my own and I'm a relatively poor man."

"Yeah? You and me both, but I forgot to marry the boss's daughter. Us cops are stupid."

I sat down and lit a cigarette. The blonde went out and closed the door.

"It's no use, is it?" I said. "I can't convince you that I'm just another guy trying to scratch a living. Do you know somebody named Lipshultz who owns a club?"

"Too well. His place is out in the desert, outside our jurisdiction. Every so often the Riverside D.A. has him raided. They say he permits gambling at his joint. I wouldn't know."

He passed his horny hand over his face and made it look like the face of a man who wouldn't know.

"He braced me in front of the office of a real estate man named Thorson. Said he was in trouble."

The sergeant stared at me expressionlessly. "Being in trouble belongs with being a man named Lipshultz. Stay away from him. Some of that trouble might rub off on you."

I stood up. "Thanks, Sergeant. I just wanted to check with you."

"You checked in. I'm looking forward to the day you check out."

I went out and closed the door. The pretty police-woman gave me a nice smile. I stopped at the desk and stared at her for a moment without speaking.

"I guess no cop ever liked a private eye," I said.

"You look all right to me, Mr. Marlowe."

"You look more than all right to me. My wife likes me part of the time too."

She leaned her elbows on the desk and clasped her hands under her chin. "What does she do the rest of the time?"

"She wishes I had ten million dollars. Then we could afford a couple more Fleetwood Cadillacs."

I grinned at her fascinatingly and went out of the cop house and climbed into our lonely Fleetwood. I struck out for the mansion.

4

At the end of the main drag the road swings to the left. To get to our place you keep straight on with nothing on the left but a hill and an occasional street on the right. A couple of tourist cars passed me going to see the palms in the State Park—as if they couldn't see all the palms they needed in Poodle Springs itself. A big Buick Roadmaster was behind me taking it easy. At a stretch of road that seemed empty it suddenly put on speed, flashed past and turned in ahead of me. I wondered what I had done wrong. Two men jumped out of the car, both very sportsclothesy, and trotted back to where I had braked to a stop. A couple of guns flashed into their busy hands. I moved my hand on the indicator enough to shift the pointer to Low. I reached for the glove compartment, but there wasn't time. They were beside the Fleetwood.

"Lippy wants to talk to you," a nasal voice snarled.

He looked like any cheap punk. I didn't bother taking an inventory of him. The other one was taller, thinner but no more delicious. But they held the guns in a casually competent manner.

"And who might Lippy be? And put the heaters away. I don't have one."

"After he spoke to you, you went to the cops. Lippy don't like that."

"Let me guess," I said brightly. "Lippy would be Mr. Lipshultz who runs or owns the Agony Club, which is out of the territory of the Poodle Springs cops and the Agony Club is engaged in extralegal operations. Why does he want to see me so badly that he has to send a couple of shnooks after me?"

"On business, big stuff."

"Naturally, I didn't think we were such close friends that he couldn't eat lunch without me."

One of the boys, the taller one, moved around behind the Fleetwood and reached for the right-hand door. It had to be now if it was going to be at all. I pushed down on the accelerator. A cheap car would have stalled, but not the Fleetwood. It shot forward and sent the taller hood reeling. It smashed hard into the rear end of the Roadmaster. I couldn't see what it did to the Fleetwood. There might be a small scratch or two on the front bumper. In the middle of the crash I yanked the glove compartment open and grabbed the .38 I had carried in Mexico, not that I had ever needed it. But when you are with Linda you don't take chances.

The smaller hood had started running. The other was still on his sitter. I hopped out of the Fleetwood and fired a shot over his head.

The other hood stopped dead, six feet away.

"Look, darlings," I said, "if Lippy wants to talk to me, he can't do it with me full of lead. And never show a gun unless you are prepared to use it. I am. You're not."

The tall boy climbed to his feet and put his gun away sullenly. After an instant the other did the same. They went to look at their car. I backed the Fleetwood clear and swung it level with the Roadmaster.

"I'll go see Lippy," I said. "He needs some advice about his staff."

"You got a pretty wife," the little hood said nastily.

"And any punk that lays a hand on her is already half cremated. So long, putrid. See you in the boneyard."

I gave the Fleetwood the gun and was out of sight. I turned into our street which like all the streets in

21

that section was a dead end between high hills bordering the mountains. I pulled up in front of the house and looked at the front of the Fleetwood. It was bent a little—not much, but too much for a lady like Linda to drive it. I went into the house and found her in the bedroom staring at dresses.

"You've been loafing," I said. "You haven't rearranged the furniture yet."

"Darling!" She threw herself at me like a medium fast pitch, high and inside. "What have you been doing?"

"I bumped your car into the back of another one. You'd better telephone for a few more Fleetwoods."

"What on earth happened? You're not a sloppy driver."

"I did it on purpose. A man named Lipshultz who runs the Agony Club braced me as I came out of a realtor's office. He wanted to talk business, but I didn't have the time then. So on my way home he had a couple of morons with guns try to persuade me to do it now. I bashed them."

"Of course you did, darling. Quite right, too. What is a realtor?"

"A real estate man with a carnation. You didn't ask me how badly damaged your car is."

"Stop calling it my car. It's our car. And I don't suppose it's damaged enough to notice. Anyhow we need a sedan for evenings. Have you had lunch?"

"You take it awfully goddamned calmly that I might have been shot."

"Well, I was really thinking about something else. I'm afraid Father will pop in soon and start buying up the town. You know how he is about publicity."

"How right he is! I've been called by name by half a dozen people already—including an exquisitely pretty blond policewoman."

"She probably knows judo," Linda said casually.

"Look, I don't get my women by violence."

"Well, perhaps. But I seem to remember being forced into somebody's bedroom."

"Force, my foot. You could hardly wait."

"Ask Tino to give you some lunch. Any more of this conversation and I'll forget I'm arranging my dresses."

5

I found an office finally, as close to a dump as Poodle Springs gets, south of Ramon Drive, upstairs over a filling station. It was the usual two-story fake adobe with make-believe ridge poles sticking out through it at the roof line. There was an outside stairway along the right wall that led to one room with a sink in the corner and a cheap deal desk left over from the previous tenant, a guy who maybe sold insurance, and maybe other stuff. Whatever he sold he didn't make enough to pay the rent, and the geezer who owned the building and ran the filling station had booted him out a month ago. Besides the desk there was a squeaky swivel chair and a grey metal file cabinet and a calendar that had a pic-

ture on it of a dog tugging down a little girl's bathing
suit bottom.

"Darling, this is appalling," Linda said when she
saw it.

"You should see some of my clients," I said.

"I could just have someone come in . . ."

"This is what I can afford," I said.

Linda nodded. "Well, I'm sure it will do very nicely,"
she said. "Now let's go out to lunch."

The phone rang. Linda picked it up.

"Philip Marlowe's office," she said. Then she listened
and wrinkled her nose and handed the phone to me.
"It must be a client, darling. He sounds appalling."

I said "Yeah" into the mouthpiece, and a voice I'd
heard before said, "Marlowe, this is Manny Lipshultz."

"How nice for you," I said.

"Okay, sending a couple of hard boys after you was
a mistake. I've made bigger."

I let that slide.

"If you're open for business I'd like to talk to you."

"Go ahead," I said.

"Can you come here?"

"The Agony Club?"

"Yeah. You know where it is?"

"Just out of Poodle Springs jurisdiction," I said.
"When?"

"Now."

"I'll be out in half an hour," I said and hung up.

Linda was looking at me with her arms folded across her chest. I let my chair squeak back and put my hands behind my head and smiled at her. She had on a ridiculous little white hat with the hint of a veil, and a sleeveless little white dress and sling strap high-heeled white shoes, the right toe of which was tapping the floor.

"I'll be out in half an hour?" she said.

"First client," I said. "I have to earn a living."

"And our lunch?"

"Call Tino, maybe he'd like to join you."

"I can't go to lunch with the houseboy."

I stood. "I'll drop you off at home."

She nodded and turned and went out of the office ahead of me. When I dropped her off she didn't kiss me good-bye, even though I went around and opened the door for her. A charmer, Marlowe. A model of courtliness.

The Agony Club was northeast of Poodle Springs, just over the line in Riverside County. A famous actor had set out to build himself a castle in the desert and then a reversal of fortune based on an incident with a 15-year-old girl, and the castle was a casualty. It looked like a bordello for wealthy Mexicans, all white stucco and red tile, with fountains in the courtyard and bougainvillaea creeping along its flanks. In the middle of the day it had a slightly tarnished look, like an over-aged screen star. There were no cars in the big crushed stone circular driveway. I could hear the hum of the air conditioner somewhere out of sight, like a locust behind the building.

I parked the Olds under the portcullis at the back of the courtyard and walked in through the cooler darkness of the entry. There were two big carved mahogany doors, one slightly ajar. I pushed through it into the suddenly cool indoors. It felt good after the hard desert heat, but it felt artificial too, like the soothing touch of an embalmer. The two hoods who'd braced me the other day appeared from somewhere to the right.

The taller one said, "You carrying?"

"Yeah," I said, "you never know when there might be something to shoot out here."

The smaller hood was only half visible, hanging back in the gloomy doorway to the right. I could see the light from the main room glint off the gun in his hand.

"Can't see Lippy with a gun," the tall one said.

I shrugged and opened my coat and the tall one took the gun smoothly from under my arm. He looked at it.

"Two-inch barrel," he said. "Not much good at a distance."

"I only work close up," I said.

The tall one led the way across the open central space. There were tables set up for blackjack, there were roulette wheels, and tables for dice. Along the far left wall was a polished mahogany bar, with bottles arranged artfully in front of a mirrored wall behind it. The only light now came from a series of tall narrow windows near the ceiling which had probably been designed to look like firing ports in the original. I could see a series of crystal chandeliers hanging unlit from the ceiling. The little hood walked five steps behind me. I didn't think he had his gun out anymore but I didn't want him to catch me looking.

At the far end of the bar three steps led up to a low landing, and a door opened off of that into a big office that belonged to Manny Lipshultz. He was in, sitting behind a desk the size of a shuffleboard court.

"Marlowe," he said. "Sit down. You want a drink?"

He got up, went around a rosewood sideboard, took a decanter from it and filled two thick chunky glasses half full. He handed me one and went around behind his desk.

"It's okay, Leonard," he said to the tall hood. "Beat it."

Leonard and his little buddy disappeared silently into the dimness. I sipped my drink, Scotch, better than I was used to, even if my wife did have ten million bucks.

"Glad you could make it, Marlowe," Lipshultz said.

"Me too," I said. "Got to make a living."

"Married to Harlan Potter's daughter?"

"That means she doesn't have to make a living," I said.

Lipshultz nodded. "I got a problem, Marlowe."

I waited.

"What we do here ain't, you know, quite legal."

"I know," I said.

"Ever wonder why we don't get the arm laid on us?"

"No," I said, "but if I did, I'd figure you had backing, and the backing had the kind of money which keeps people from getting the arm laid on them."

Lipshultz smiled. "Smart, Marlowe. I knew you was smart even before I had you checked out."

"So with that kind of connection, what do you need me for?"

Lipshultz shook his head sadly. He had a thick nose to go with his red face, and slick black hair parted in the middle and combed tight on each side of his bullet head.

"Can't use that backing in this," he said. "Fact if you don't help me out, the backing is going to maybe send some people out to see me, you follow?"

"If they do you should get better help than the two yahoos you got following you around now."

"That's the truth," Lippy said. "Hard to get people to come out here, I mean this ain't Los Angeles. Not everybody likes the desert. Why I was so glad when I found out you was here. I heard about you when you were operating out of Hollywood."

"Your lucky day," I said. "What do you want me to do?"

He handed me an IOU for $100,000, with the signature *Les Valentine* across the bottom in a neat, very small hand. Then he sat back to let that sink in.

"Me," Lippy said, "taking a guy's marker for a hundred g's. I must be getting old."

"How come you did?" I said.

"He had money in the family. Always made good before."

"And when Mr. Big that runs you audited the books one day he noticed you were $ 100,000 short."

"His bookkeeper," Lipshultz said. "And Mr. Blackstone came to see me."

The air-conditioned room was full of cold, but Lipshultz was sweating. He pulled the silk show handkerchief from his pocket and wiped his neck with it.

"Drove right out here himself and sat where you're sitting and told me I had thirty days to cover the loss," Lipshultz said.

"Or?"

"There ain't no 'or' with Mr. Blackstone, Marlowe."

"So you want me to find the guy who stuck you."

Lipshultz nodded.

"I find people, Lipshultz, I don't shake them down."

"That's all I'm asking you, Marlowe. I'm out a hundred grand. I don't get it back and I'm dead. You find the guy. Talk to him."

"What if he doesn't have it? Guys that lose a hundred g's at the tables don't usually have it for long," I said.

"He's got it. His wife's worth twenty, thirty million."

"So why not ask her?"

"I have, she don't believe me. She says her Lester wouldn't do that. And I say ask Lester, and she says he's away now, doing stills for some movie shooting north of L.A."

"How come you didn't shake her down?"

Lipshultz shook his head. "She's a lady," he said.

"And you're a gentleman," I said.

Lipshultz shrugged. "What the hell," he said.

I believed that like I believed you should draw to an inside straight, but there didn't seem to be anything for me in arguing about it.

"I'll pay you ten percent if you get the money," Lipshultz said.

"I get a hundred dollars a day and expenses," I said.

Lipshultz nodded. "Heard you was a boy scout."

"There's some people doing twenty to life in San Quentin thought the same thing," I said.

Lipshultz grinned. "Heard you thought you was tough, too."

"Where do I find this guy?" I said.

"Valentine, Les Valentine. Lives with his wife somewhere in Poodle Springs, out near the Racquet Club. Want me to look it up?"

"I'm a trained sleuth," I said. "I'll look it up. Can I keep the IOU?"

"Sure," Lipshultz said. "I got copies."

Lipshultz gave me $100 as a retainer and pushed a button somewhere because Leonard and his alter ego showed up. Leonard gave me back my gun, alter ego stayed far enough away so I wouldn't bite him and followed me out through the gambling layout and into the hot bright daylight at the front door. He and Leonard watched while I got into the Olds and drove away with the hot wind washing over me through the open windows.

6

Les Valentine's house was off Racquet Club Road, on one of those curvy little streets created to make an instant neighborhood. There were giant cactus plants at regular intervals, and jacaranda trees for a touch of color. The bungalows with their wide roofs were set close to the drive so that there was room for the pool in back, and the patio, which represented the ultimate advancement of civilization in the desert. No one was in sight. The only movement was the soft sluice of water sprinklers. Everybody was probably inside trying on outfits for the party at the Racquet Club Saturday night.

I parked the Olds in front and walked up the

crushed white stone path to the porch. On either side of the Spanish oak door there were bull's-eye glass panels which went with the Spanish architecture like a Scotch Margarita. A Japanese houseboy opened the door and took my hat and put me in the front parlor to sit while he went for Madame.

The room was all white stucco. In one corner was a conical stucco fireplace in case the temperature dropped below ninety after the sun went down. The hearth was red Mexican tile. On the front wall was a large oil painting of a mean-looking guy in a three-piece suit with big white eyebrows, and the mouth of a man who tips people a nickel. On the end wall, to the left of the fireplace, was a series of photographs, full of arty lighting from below and odd over-the-shoulder poses of women. Black and white stuff, framed expensively as if they were important. On an easel near the doors to the patio was a big blow-up of a man and a woman. She was in her mid-30s, serious-looking, with the same kind of mouth as the mean-looking old guy in the oil on the front wall. Even though he was balding, the man with her seemed younger. He wore rimless glasses in the picture and a smile that said, *Don't pay attention to me.*

"Mr. Marlowe?"

I turned to look at the woman from the picture.

She was frowning down at the brand-new card I'd had printed up. I hadn't even had an office yet when I ordered them so they merely said *Philip Marlowe, Investigation, Poodle Springs*. Linda had vetoed the brass knuckles rampant.

"Yes, Ma'am," I said.

"Sit down, please," she said. "Have you been admiring my husband's work?"

"Yes, Ma'am. Is that your husband with you here?" I nodded at the picture.

"Yes, that's Les. He set the timer and then joined me. He's very clever."

The body belied the face. The face with its penurious mouth said, *I won't give you a damned thing.* The body with strong breasts and proud hips said, *You can have anything you can take.* I was newly married to an angel, but I could feel the challenge.

"That's my father in the painting," she said.

I smiled.

"You may smoke, if you wish," she said. "I do not, my father never approved, but Les does and I rather enjoy the smell."

"Thanks," I said. "Maybe in a while."

I crossed my legs.

"I'm trying to locate your husband, Mrs. Valentine."

"Really?'"

"Yes, I've been employed to find him by a man who claims your husband owes him $100,000."

"That's ridiculous."

"My employer says that your husband ran up $100,000 in gambling debts at his, ah, casino and left him holding IOU's for the amount."

"IOU's for illegal gambling are not enforceable," she snapped.

"Yes, Ma'am. But it has put my client in a difficult position with his employer."

"Mr. Marlowe, this is no doubt of interest to someone. But surely not to me, or to anyone who knows my husband. My husband does not gamble. Nor does he give people IOU's. He pays for what he buys. He does not need to do otherwise. He makes a good living, and I am the fortunate recipient of my father's considerable generosity."

"Could you tell me where your husband is now, Ma'am? Perhaps if I talked with him I could clear this up."

"Les is on location in San Benedict with a film company. He is doing publicity photographs. Studios often employ him for that sort of thing. He is a very accomplished and well-regarded photographer of young women."

She liked the young women part the way a cow likes beefsteak.

"I see that," I said. "Which studio is he working for?"

Mrs. Valentine shrugged, as if the question were negligible. "I don't keep track," she said.

When she wasn't speaking she kept her lips slightly apart and her tongue moved restlessly in her mouth. "And I am certainly not going to have him beset with some wild accusations from a man known to be a criminal."

"I didn't say who my employer was," I said.

"I know who it is, it's that Mr. Lipshultz. He approached me directly and I let him know then what I thought of his cock-and-bull story."

I took Lippy's IOU out of my inside pocket and held it up for her to see.

She shook her head angrily. "He showed me that, too," she said. "I don't believe it. It's not Les's signature."

I got up and walked to one of the artsy framed photographs on the wall. In the lower right corner they were signed *Les Valentine* in the same innocuous cramped little hand that I had on the IOU. I held the IOU signature beside the photo signature. I held the pose for a minute with my eyebrows raised.

She stared at the two signatures as if she'd never seen either one. Her tongue darted about in her mouth. She was breathing a little harder than she had been.

She rose suddenly and walked to the bleached oak sideboard under her father's picture.

"I will have a drink, Mr. Marlowe. Would you care to join me?"

"No, Ma'am," I said, "but I'll smoke my cigarette now, I think."

I shook one loose and lipped it out of the pack. I lit it and drew in a lungful of smoke and let it out slowly through my nose. Mrs. Valentine poured herself some kind of green liquor and sipped it two or three quick times before she turned back to me.

"My husband enjoys gambling, Mr. Marlowe. I know that, and I hoped to prevent you from knowing that."

I worked on my cigarette a little while she drank most of the rest of her green drink.

"I have been happy to indulge him in this . . . my father would have said weakness, I suppose. As I say, I enjoy my father's affection and his largesse. Les is an artistic man, and like many artists he is whimsical. He is full of quirky needs. Sensitivities, one might say, that other men, perhaps like you, worldly men, do not necessarily have. In the past I have paid his debts and

39

been happy to have contributed in my way to his artistic fulfillment."

She went back to the sideboard and poured herself another drink. It looked like something she did easily. She drank some.

"But this, $100,000 to a man like Lipshultz." She shook her head as if she couldn't continue, or saw no need to. "We talked, I said that it was time for him to become responsible, to grow a bit more worldly. I hoped, frankly, to snap him out of his childishness in this regard. I said he would have to liquidate this debt himself."

I finished my cigarette and stubbed it out in a polished abalone shell that sat on the end table in the middle of the desert. I looked at the photographs of young women on the wall. I wondered how many sensitivities Les had to be indulged in.

"Does he work out of his home?" I said.

The bilious hooch she was drinking was beginning to work. She shifted her hips restlessly as she stood by the sideboard. Her thighs beneath the black silk lounging slacks were full of energy. There was a smudge of red along the high cheekbones on the schoolmarm face.

"Like a part-time plumber? Hardly. He has an office in Los Angeles."

"Do you have the address, Mrs. Valentine?"

"Certainly not. Les comes and goes as he will. Our marriage is perfectly founded on trust. I don't need to know his office address."

I let my eyes run over the glamour photos mounted on the wall. Several of the women were famous, two movie stars, one a model who'd been on the cover of *Life*. All were signed in the lower right corner in gold in the distinctive small hand.

Mrs. Valentine was watching me. Her glass was nearly full again.

"You think I fear those women, Mr. Marlowe? You think I can't keep him at home?"

She put her drink on the sideboard and half turned so I could see her in partial profile and ran her hands over her breasts and down along her body, smoothing the fabric on her thighs.

"Zowie," I said.

She stared at me, holding the pose, the dark rose color spreading across her cheeks. Then she chuckled, a nasty, bubbly little sound.

"The $100,000 is a matter between you and Les and that dreadful Mr. Lipshultz. If you want to play your little boy games, go ahead. I will await the . . ." she made a gentle hiccup ". . . outcome." She sipped her drink.

"What is that stuff?" I said. "It smells like plant food."

"Good-bye, Mr. Marlowe."

I stood, put on my hat and went out of there. She was still posing with her chest stuck out. There was a big potted palm tree on the front porch. I looked at it as I went by.

"Maybe she'll give you some," I said.

7

Tino was at the door when I pulled the Olds in beside Linda's Fleetwood.

"Mrs. Marlowe is by the pool, sir."

"Thank you, Tino, how does she look?"

"Very lovely, sir."

"That's correct, Tino."

Tino smiled widely. I went through the make-believe living room and out onto the patio by the pool. Linda was on a pale blue chaise, wearing a one-piece white bathing suit and a pale blue wide-brimmed hat that matched the chaise. On the low white table next to the chaise a tall narrow glass contained something with fruit in it. Linda looked up from her book.

"Darling, have you had a hard day talking with Mr. Lipshultz?"

I took off my coat and loosened my tie. I sat in the pale blue chair beside the chaise. Linda ran one fingernail along the crease of my pants.

"Did my big detective get all worn out working all day?"

Tino appeared at the patio door.

"May I bring you something, sir?"

I smiled gratefully.

"A gimlet," I said. "Make it a double."

Tino nodded and disappeared.

"I talked to Lipshultz," I said. "I also talked to Mrs. Les Valentine."

Linda raised her eyebrows. "Muffy Blackstone?"

"Woman maybe forty-five," I said. "Looks like someone pasted the head of a schoolteacher on the body of a Varga girl."

"That's Muffy. Though I'm not sure I like you noticing the body."

"Just doing my job," I said.

"She's Clayton Blackstone's daughter. He's a friend of Daddy's. Very wealthy. At forty she married for the first time, a nobody. The Springs was in an uproar."

"What do you know about Les?"

"Very little. No money, no distinction. It is assumed

he married her for her money. Clayton Blackstone is perhaps wealthier than Daddy."

"Heavens," I said.

"He seems quite a drab little man," Linda said.

"Yeah," I said. "Probably has a run-down office someplace, over a garage."

"Oh, darling," Linda said. "Don't be such a bastard."

Tino appeared with a large square glass set on a squat stem. He took it carefully off the tray and set it down on a napkin by my elbow. He looked at Linda's glass, noticed it was nearly full and went silently away.

"What does Clayton Blackstone do?" I said.

"He is wealthy," she said. "That's what he does."

"Like your daddy," I said.

Linda smiled brightly. I sipped some of the gimlet. It was clean and cold and slid down through the desert parch like a fresh rain.

"Hard to make all that money," I said, "without getting your hands a little dirty."

"Daddy never said that."

"No, I'll bet he didn't."

"Why do you say that? What are you doing talking to Muffy Blackstone?"

"Valentine."

"Muffy Valentine."

I drank another swallow of the gimlet. The pool glistened blue and still beside me.

"Her husband is into Lippy for a hundred g's."

"Into?"

"Lippy took his marker. Mrs. Valentine had always bailed him out before. This time she won't. Says he's got to grow up, and settle this debt himself."

"Well, good for her. I'm sure he's been a dreadful trial."

"She seems a little trying herself," I said.

"Yes, I suppose she is," Linda said. A beautiful frown wrinkle appeared briefly between her eyebrows. I leaned over and kissed it. "She was single all that time and devoted to Daddy, and all . . . She drinks a little too much, too."

"Anyway. Guy Lippy works for is unhappy about getting stuck for a hundred g's, told Lippy he had thirty days to get it back. Lippy can't find Les. Mrs. Valentine says he's off doing still work on a picture set. Lippy says if he doesn't get it back his boss will send a couple of hard boys out to see him. So Lippy hired me to find Les and talk him into giving Lippy his hundred thousand."

"Well, if anyone can do it, I'm sure you can. Look how you've been able to talk me right out of my clothes," Linda said.

"As I recall I don't get the chance to," I said. I looked at the pool. "Have you ever . . . ?"

"In a pool?" Linda said. "Darling, you are a beast. Besides, what about Tino?"

"I don't care if Tino's ever done anything in a pool," I said.

We each drank a little bit of our drink. The desert evening was already cooling, and the desert sounds were starting to dwindle. I listened to it for a while, looking at the arch of Linda's foot. Linda listened too.

"Funny thing," I said after a while, "the big boss, guy was going to put the heat on Lippy. His name was Blackstone."

"Clayton Blackstone?"

"I don't know. Probably a different Blackstone."

"Oh, I'm sure," Linda said.

Tino came in a little while with two more drinks on a tray. He took away the empty glasses and was gone as silently as he'd come. Except when he served you it was as if he didn't exist. High up a prairie hawk moved in slow circles, riding the wind's currents, its spread wings nearly motionless.

"Why would you do this, darling? Work for this man Lipshultz?"

"It's my profession," I said.

"Even though you don't need the money?"

47

I sighed. "You don't need the money. I do. I don't have any put aside."

"But a man like Lipshultz?"

"In my business you don't get all well-bred upper-class people who have good manners and live in safe neighborhoods," I said. "In my kind of work Lipshultz is well above average."

"Then why not get into another business?" Linda said.

"I like my work," I said.

"I'm sure Daddy would . . ."

I cut her off. "Sure he could, and I could get a grey flannel suit and be the boss's son-in-law, except I'm kind of old to be the boss's son-in-law."

Linda looked away.

"Look," I said, "Mrs. Marlowe. I'm just a lug. There are things I can do. I can shoot, I can keep my word, I can walk into dark narrow places. So I do them. I find work that fits what I do, and who I am. Manny Lipshultz is in trouble, he can pay, he's not hiring me to do something illegal, or even immoral. He's in trouble and he needs help and that's what I do and he's got money and I need some. Would you be happier if I took Mrs. Valentine's money to help her husband welch on his debt?"

"I'd rather we stopped talking about this and went in

and had dinner and then retired to our room and . . ." She shrugged her shoulders in a way that didn't mean *I don't know.*

"You're very demanding, Mrs. Marlowe."

"Yes," she said, "I am."

We went in and left the glasses where they were. What the hell. Tino would pick them up. Didn't want the help getting bored.

8

There were 55 Valentines in the L.A. phone book. One was a Lester and one was a Leslie. Lester lived in Encino and was a Division Manager for Pacific Bell; Leslie had a place on Hope Street and was a retail florist. I called information. They hadn't any other Les Valentines listed.

I had no office in L.A. anymore. I had to make the calls from a phone booth on the corner of Cahuenga and Hollywood Boulevard across from the old office. I called a local modeling agency and the Chamber of Commerce in San Benedict. They were both civil to me, which is a high average in L.A.

It was January and cool in L.A. Across the valley,

the highest peaks of the San Gabriel Mountains were snow-capped. In Hollywood people pretended it was winter and wore furs along the boulevard, and producers wore argyle sweaters under tweed jackets on their way to lunch at Musso and Frank's. I was clean-shaven, smelling of bay rum and back in town for the first time in a month. Fast, tough, and on a case.

I got in the Olds, went south a block to Sunset and then headed west.

The Triton Modeling Agency was in a courtyard off of Westwood Boulevard, just north of Olympic. The center of the courtyard was covered with white pebbles divided into squares with redwood planking. In each square a small palm tree grew in single file down the center of the yard. There were maybe ten commercial establishments in the complex, a rare-book shop, a store selling Mexican jewelry, a leather store, a lawyer. I walked along the low-canopied porch that fronted the entries until I came to Triton. I rang the little brass bell and opened the door. It was a plush, carpeted silver office. Walls and ceiling done in silver paint, the reception desk silver plastic, and behind the desk a blonde with long thighs and flawless nylons. She wore a scarlet dress of some loose knit material, and as I entered she was reapplying scarlet color to her lips. She kept carefully at it while I stood in front of her desk.

"Yippie I oh chi yea," I said.

She finished her last touch and closed her compact mirror and looked at me.

"Yes, Cowboy?"

"I'm easily excited," I said.

"How nice for you," she said.

"Married, too," I said.

"How nice for you," she said.

"Thanks. My name is Marlowe. I called about one of your models, Sondra Lee?"

"Ah, the detective." She looked me over the way a fish examines a worm. "Well, you've certainly got the shoulders for it," she said.

"Can you tell me how to get in touch with Miss Lee?" I said.

"Sure," the blonde said. "I called her. She said you can come see her at her place."

The blonde handed me a piece of paper with an address on it.

"It's off Beverly Glen," the blonde said. "Near the top."

I thanked her and turned to leave.

"If the marriage doesn't work . . ." she said.

I turned, gave her the gunman's salute with my thumb and forefinger, and left.

I picked up Beverly Glen off of Wilshire. North of

Sunset it started to climb. The foliage pressed in close on it and the hills rose on either side waiting for the first heavy rain to wash the houses that rode their flanks down into the roadway. Sondra Lee's place would be one of the first to go. Its back end rested on two 15-foot lally columns that stood on concrete footings in the hillside. The driveway curved around the house and stopped to form a circle in front. There was no yard but the area in front of the house was full of flowering shrubs, and hummingbirds danced and spiraled over them as I pulled the car to a stop near the front door.

A Mexican woman answered my ring. Miss Lee was in the solarium. I followed her through the overdone bungalow into a glass addition that leaned against the front side of the house. A door at one end opened out onto the pool. It was closed now against the bite of a Hollywood winter, and Miss Lee was reclining indoors, on a leather-covered fainting couch, wearing a very small two-piece black bathing suit and tanning in the rays of the afternoon sun as it came filtering through the glass roof. There was a bar across the end nearest the house, and a couple of canvas chairs sitting about.

The woman on the couch had been on so many magazine covers that I felt I knew her. Her hair was jet black, and her eyes were black, and her skin was pale even after tanning. She looked like you could disappear forever into one of her sighs.

"Miss Lee," I said, "I'm Philip Marlowe."

"Of course, Mr. Marlowe. I've been expecting you. Will you have a drink?"

I said I would.

She smiled slowly and nodded toward the bar.

"Please help yourself, I really need to get another fifteen minutes of sun," she said. She had a way of dragging out every word so that she spoke very slowly, and you were obliged to hang on her words. I made a tall Scotch at the bar, adding ice from the silver bucket and watching the moisture bead up on the glass in the warm room.

I took my drink and sat in one of the canvas chairs where she could see me. I tried not to stare at her.

"I saw your photograph yesterday, hanging in the hallway of a man's home," I said. "He is a photographer and you had posed for him."

"Oh? What is his name?" she said.

"Valentine," I said. "Les Valentine."

She reached to the table beside her and took a long pull on a glass half full of what looked like water but probably wasn't.

"Valentine," she said. "What was his first name?"

"Les, that's how he signed the photograph, in gold, down in the right-hand corner."

"Les," she said. She shook her head slowly and nibbled a little more from her glass.

"I don't know any Les," she said.

"You get photographed so much," I said. "It must be hard to remember."

She shook her head and buried her muzzle in the glass again. When she came up for air she said, "No. I only let a few people photograph me. I would know if anyone took my picture."

She shifted slightly as if in keeping with the slow slide of the sun in the western sky, her nearly still body absorbing all it could get like some kind of gorgeous lizard. She emptied her glass and held it out toward me.

"Be a darling," she said, "and freshen my glass."

I took it and went to the bar.

"The cut glass decanter, at the far right," she said.

I took it, took out the stopper and poured her glass nearly full. I took a discreet sniff as I poured. Vodka. No wonder she talked slowly. I put the stopper back and brought her the drink.

"So why would a guy named Les Valentine have a photograph of you to which he'd signed his name?" I said.

"Because he wishes people to think he has photographed me, but he has not."

"Because you are famous," I said.

She was making good progress on her refilled glass.

"Of course. It makes people think he is important. But he is not. If he were important I would know him."

"And he you," I said.

She smiled at me as if we knew the secret to eternal health.

"I'll bet you have big muscles," she said.

"No bigger than Bronco Nagurski," I said.

"Do you think I'm beautiful?" she said.

I nodded. She drank a little more of her drink and put the glass down and smiled at me.

"I think you're beautiful too," she said. "But you have not seen everything." She twisted suddenly and put her hands behind her back and unhitched her bra strap, then she rolled over and arched and with the same quick grace she slid out of the bikini bottoms. Then she lay back against the chaise again and smiled at me, her pale tan body naked as a salamander.

"Dandy," I said.

She continued to smile and stretched her arms out toward me.

"Have I told you about Mrs. Marlowe?" I said.

She smiled even more brightly.

"You are married." She shrugged. "I am married." She beckoned again with her arms.

I took a cigarette out and put it in my mouth and let it hang there unlit.

"Look, Mrs. Lee . . ." I started.

"Mrs. Ricardo," she said. "Lee is my maiden name. So you may call me Miss Lee, or Mrs. Ricardo, you see. But you can't call me Mrs. Lee."

"Fine," I said. "You are very attractive, and I am very male, and seeing you there rolling around in the nude has the usual effect. But I usually like to spend a little more time getting to know the women I sleep with, and being as I'm married and all, I only sleep with my wife."

I took the unlit cigarette out of my mouth and rolled it between my fingers. We both looked at it.

"Which I do often," I said.

There was a fat round silver and pigskin table lighter on the end table near her chaise. I reached over and picked it up. I put the cigarette back in my mouth and lit it. When I looked up from doing that, I saw a tall man with a very strong nose standing in the doorway. I exhaled smoke slowly.

"What the hell?" the tall guy said. He had high

shoulders and black hair slicked back smoothly from a widow's peak and hard dark eyes that glimmered on either side of the hatchet nose.

"Tommy," Sondra Lee said, not even looking. She took a delicate taste of her vodka. "Mr. Marlowe was admiring how beautiful I am."

"I can see that," Tommy said.

"Mr. Marlowe, this is my husband, Tommy Ricardo."

I nodded politely.

"Okay, pal," Ricardo said. "On your way, and quick."

On the chaise Sondra Lee giggled and wiggled herself a little.

"For chrissake, Sonny, cover yourself," Ricardo said, then his glance came back to me. I was still sitting, considering my cigarette.

"On your way, I told you once, pally. I'm not going to tell you again."

"Sure," I said. "You're tougher than a sackful of carpet tacks. She do this often?"

"She's a lush," he said. "She does it a lot. On your feet."

He took two steps toward me and his right hand came out of the pocket of his plaid madras sport coat. He had brass knuckles on it.

"Does this mean we're engaged?" I said.

He took another step and I was on my feet just in time to pull my chin out of the way of the knucks as they glittered past it. I stepped in under the right arm that was extended past me, slipped my left arm under his left arm and got a full nelson on him and held it.

"My name's Marlowe," I said. "I'm a private detective, and I came here to ask your wife about an entirely unrelated matter."

Ricardo was breathing hard. But he wasn't struggling. He knew I had him and he was waiting.

"Unrelated to what," he said in a half-strangled voice.

"Unrelated to her getting soused and taking off her clothes."

"You son of a bitch," he gasped.

"Taking them off wasn't my idea. She looks good, but I've got a wife who looks better, and when you showed up I was telling her that."

From the chaise, Lee was still giggling. There was real excitement in the giggle now. I looked over. She was still buck naked.

"Mrs. Ricardo, do you know anything at all about a guy named Les Valentine?" I said.

She shook her head slowly. Her eyes were wide and

the pupils were very dilated. Maybe there was more than vodka in the decanter.

"Okay," I said. I bent Ricardo farther forward with the nelson. Then I put my knee against his backside, let go the nelson and shoved with my knee. He went forward stumbling three or four steps, and by the time he was able to get his balance I was out of the solarium and heading through the living room. I wasn't carrying a gun. I hadn't figured to need one at the top of Beverly Glen. He didn't come after me and I was out the door and in my Olds and heading downhill, with the sound of her giggle still ringing in my ear.

It was five o'clock and the traffic back into the Valley from L.A. streamed past me. The lights in the houses began to flick on, making sort of a Christmas tree effect in the dark hills. Sondra Lee's home probably looked just as pretty as the others now, in the early evening, with the darkness gathering. They knew something out here. You could make anything look good with the right lighting.

9

The three-hour drive back to Poodle Springs was more than I could face, so I had a steak in a joint on La Cienega and bedded down in a roach trap on Hollywood Boulevard, where the bed would vibrate for a minute if you put a quarter in the slot. There was no room service, but the clerk said he could sell me a half pint of bonded rye for a buck.

I sipped a little of the rye while I talked on the phone to Linda. Then I fell asleep and dreamed of a cave with a cross-beamed door that stood half open and from the darkness came a giggle endlessly repeating.

In the morning I showered and shaved, ate eggs and toast at Schwab's counter and drank three cups of coffee. I loaded my pipe, got it fired, climbed into the Olds and drove through Laurel Canyon. I picked up 101 in Ventura and headed west through the Santa Monica Mountains and then north along the coast.

San Benedict looks like tourists think California looks. It is full of white stuccoed houses and red tile roofs. The Pacific rolls in flatly along its ocean front where palm trees grow sedately in a long, orderly park.

The Chamber of Commerce was in a cluster of Spanish-type buildings that looked like somebody's idea of a hacienda, about two blocks uphill from the ocean front. The bald guy manning the office had on arm garters and suspenders and smoked a noxious cigar that was obviously not worth the nickel he'd spent on it.

"My name's Marlowe," I said. "I called yesterday asking if there was a movie company shooting here."

Baldy took the cigar out of his mouth and said, "Yep, logged that call in myself. Right here." He looked down proudly at an open ledger. "NDN Pictures shooting something called *Dark Adventure*. I told you."

"Yes, sir," I said. "Could you tell me where they are today?"

"Absolutely, Bub. We make 'em tell us every day, so

we can steer people away from the traffic, or toward the set, depending on what they want."

"Smart," I said.

"Which do you want?" he said.

"Toward the set."

"Shooting today." He consulted a batch of papers on his desk. All the papers were clipped together with a big metal spring clip. He licked his thumb. "They're shooting today . . ." He thumbed several papers, licked his thumb again, came to a mimeographed sheet, studied it a moment. "Shooting at the corner of Sequoia and Esmeralda. It's a playground."

He looked up at me with a big friendly smile, shifted the cigar to the other corner of his mouth. His teeth when he smiled around the cigar were yellow.

"Down the hill, left along the water, 'bout six blocks, can't miss 'em. Damn trucks and trailers and things all over the place."

I said thank you and went out and drove back down the hill and turned left and drove along the water. He was right. I couldn't miss them.

I parked behind a truck full of electrical gear and walked into the location. Every time I went to where they were shooting film I was struck by how easy the access is. Nobody asked who I was. Nobody told me to get out of the way. Nobody offered me a screen test.

I stopped a guy at the commissary truck. He wore no shirt and his sunburned belly sagged out over his chino shorts.

"Who's in charge around here?" I said.

"Hell of a question," he said. "You from the studio?"

"No, I'm just looking for a guy. Who do I talk to about staff?"

The fat man shrugged. "Producer's Joe King," he said.

"Where do I find him?" I said.

"Last I seen him he's down by the cameras talking to the UPM." The fat guy had a paper cup of coffee in each hand and gestured with his belly in the direction of the cameras.

"Where you see all the lights," he said.

I walked where he told me to, picking my way over the tangle of cables and around light stands and generators. The crew had probably arrived with the morning dew because the ground was muddied and the grass had been churned into the mud by the equipment and the men setting it up. Movies made a mess even before they were shot.

There were several men grouped behind the cameras while the Director of Photography fiddled with the lighting.

"Which one of you is Joe King?" I said.

A tall young guy turned toward me. He was loose jointed and moved easily and there seemed to be a great natural calmness in him. He wore horn-rimmed glasses, and the sleeves of his white dress shirt were rolled above the elbows.

"I'm Joe," he said.

I showed him the photostat of my California license, inside the celluloid holder in my wallet.

"Name's Marlowe," I said. "Looking for a photographer named Les Valentine."

King looked carefully at my license, then looked up at me, friendly as an alderman at a picnic.

"Can't say I know him," King said.

"I was led to believe he was here, on assignment, shooting the stills."

King shook his head. "No, we have a regular studio photographer who does that for us. Name's Gus Johnson. I don't know any Les Val . . . whatever."

"If he were here would you know it?"

"Certainly."

"Thank you," I said.

"Care to stay, watch a little of the shooting? The star is Elayna St. Cyr."

"I have a picture of Theda Bara in my car. I'll look at it on the ride back."

King shrugged and turned back to the camera and I headed back to my car.

There were several things I thought as I drove back down the coast. The most important one was that Les Valentine was not who his wife said he was. Or who he said he was. He didn't have an office in L.A. He hadn't photographed Sondra Lee. He wasn't shooting stills on a movie being shot in San Benedict. After two days hot on his trail I knew less than I had when I started.

10

I'd been watching Muffy Valentine's house for a week, sitting in my car with the air conditioning on and the motor idling, building up carbon deposits in my cylinders. Every morning Muffy came out wearing a light raincoat over lavender tights and headed off to her exercise class. Two minutes later the Japanese houseboy came out of the house with two toy poodles straining on the leash and yapping, turned down the drive and walked off around the bend. Each day he returned with them about five minutes after his employer returned from exercising.

After three days of this I followed him around the bend and watched him go in the front door of another house, poodles and all. He stayed in there for 45 minutes and when he came out I got a quick glimpse of a Japanese housemaid closing the door behind him. About twenty minutes later a woman with platinum hair and pink tights pulled up in a silver Mercedes and strolled into the house. Even from a distance I could see the light glinting on her diamonds.

I thought carefully on these matters and the following Monday, while Muffy and her neighbor were at exercise class and the houseboy was playing Japanese Sandman with his countrywoman, I set out to B&E Muffy's house.

I had a clipboard I'd picked up downtown in the Springs, and a yellow pad on it, and a pencil behind my ear. That normally is enough to get you into the President's bedroom, unquestioned, but to make doubly sure I carried a tape measure on my belt. A tape measure combined with a clipboard will get you in while the President and First Lady are locked in carnal embrace. I parked out front of the Valentine house, walked up the front walk like a man with money in his pocket and measured the front door while I checked what kind of lock there was. It was a Bulger. I put the tape measure back on my belt, took out a collection of master keys I'd collected over the years and, on the second try, opened the front door. I put the keys back, checked along the hinges and the lock, took one more measurement, which was mostly showing off, and went in. There was no sound. If there was an alarm it was silent. If the cops showed up I'd deal with that when it happened. I was a hot shot from L.A., what had I to fear from the law in Poodle Springs? I checked my watch. I had about fifty minutes.

The front parlor yielded nothing I hadn't seen already, the dining room was just a dining room, neither had anyplace where clues might be stored. Neither did the kitchen. I went down the long hallway that ran across the back wing of the house and found their bedroom. I knew it was theirs because there were some men's suits in the closet, but the rest was hers. A huge pink canopied bed with a thick pink down comforter, maybe twenty-five pillows in white and pink. A long dressing table stood along the wall parallel to the bed. It was made out of some kind of pale wood, unpainted, but sealed with something that made it shine. There were bottles of perfume, containers of lipstick and rouge, mascara, eye shadow, wrinkle cream, hand cream and maybe thirty other items that I didn't recognize, though I'd seen some like them in Linda's bathroom. The drapes were pink and billowed out over the floor as if the decorator had made them five feet too long. The walls were white and there were two closets, one on either side of a very large dresser. The closet doors were pink, glazed with a whitewash which gave them a streaky antique look. There was a night table on either side of the bed with very large lamps of hammered copper on them. The shades were pink. Neither night table had a drawer in it.

The only drawers in the room were in the bureau. The top drawer contained women's lingerie in a tangle of pastel silk. In the far back corner under the tangle was an electric vibrator and a tube of KY jelly. I almost blushed, except that I was a hardened big-city gumshoe. In the second drawer were blouses, in the third were stockings and gloves. In the fourth were sweaters. In the bottom drawer were some men's shirts, socks, underwear. Nothing fancy. On the top of the bureau was a pink and white striped box about the size of a cigar box, and another, matching, nearly the size of a case of beer. The small one contained a pair of gold and turquoise cuff links, a tie clasp that matched, a gold collar pin. There was also a checkbook, a nail clipper, and a small bottle of eye drops. I pocketed the checkbook. The bigger box was full of jewelry. The two coat closets were full of women's dresses, plus about six men's suits, or suit coats and slacks, neatly hung together in coordination. There was a tie rack inside the closet door holding a dozen or so silk ties in most of the primary colors. Way in the back of the left-hand closet, behind the dresses, were several frothy and slightly comic see-through kinds of nightwear, black lace, white gossamer, like a young girl's idea of sexy.

Down the hall farther were two guest rooms, and two baths. The guest rooms and one of the bathrooms looked sterilely unused. I looked at my watch. Time was up. I went down the stairs, closed the front door behind me, made sure it had locked, strolled down the walk, got into my Olds and was driving away well within the speed limit when I passed Muffy barely peeping over the dashboard of her enormous black Chrysler coming around the curve in the opposite direction. She paid me no attention, having all she could do to pilot the Chrysler.

My office over the gas station wasn't air conditioned. When I opened the door it was like walking into a pizza oven. But it didn't smell as good. I left the door open and went over and turned on the oscillating fan I'd brought from L.A. when I closed my office in the Cahuenga building. The hot air moved the sweat around on my face, as I sat at my desk and looked at the checkbook. Not much for committing a felony punishable by one to five in Soledad.

The checkbook was Valentine's, not joint, just Lester A. Valentine and the address imprinted on the checks.

He showed a current balance of $7,754.66. I went through the ledger part of the book. It dated back to the previous November 8. There were entries for photographic equipment, for some men's clothing, quite a number for cash, dues at the Racquet Club, a monthly bill from Melvin's at the Poodle Springs Hotel and Resort Center, and a parking ticket made out to Parking Clerk, City of Los Angeles, and the ticket number. It was the only thing in the checkbook that didn't connect him to Poodle Springs. I decided it was a clue. I copied down the check number and the ticket number and put the checkbook in my desk and locked the drawer and got out the bottle of Scotch that I kept in my desk in case I was bitten by a Gila monster. I poured myself a small snort and sipped it and thought about why a guy would go off and leave behind him a checkbook carrying a balance of more than $7,500.

I finished my drink and poured another one. There were no Gila monsters in sight, but you never knew.

11

We had our first open house of the winter season, or
Linda did. I tried to stay out of the way. And failed. At
5:30 when the first guests arrived I was there wearing
a white jacket that Linda loved and I didn't. As people
came in Linda acted as if they were more welcome than
a cool shower in August. I knew for a fact she despised
at least one in three. My average was higher and it grew
as the night wore on.

There were probably two hundred people. Tino
tended bar, beautiful in a tuxedo that fit him the way
clothes only fit Asian houseboys. The caterer's people
moved balletically among the throngs, bearing silver

trays of champagne and edible doodads. I leaned on the bar, nursing a Scotch.

"So you're the new hubby," a woman said to me.

"I prefer 'current heartthrob,' " I said.

"Of course you do," the woman said. "My name's Mousy Fairchild. Linda and I have known each other for nearly ever, for a couple of very young women."

The thing I noticed first about her was that she smelled of rain-washed flowers, and the second that her pale violet silk gown clung to her like the skin clings to a grape. Her hair was blonder than God had ever intended, and her skin was darkly and evenly tanned which made her perfect teeth seem even whiter when she smiled. Her lips were touched with the same color as her dress and the lower lip was quite full and looked as if it was designed to be nibbled on.

"Would you like something besides the fizzy grape juice?" I said.

"Oh, you are a dear. Yes, I'll have a vodka martini on the rocks with a twist," she said. "Shaken first."

I looked at Tino. He was already mixing the martini. Tino was a boy who wasted no time not listening.

"Be a dear," Mousy said, "make it a double."

Tino smiled as if never had he enjoyed such a pleasure and added more vodka to the shaker.

"Do you have a cigarette?" she said.

I produced a pack and shook one loose.

"My God," she said. "A Camel? If I smoke that I may faint."

She took it and leaned toward me while I held a match for her. When it was lit she stayed leaning toward me and sucked in the smoke while she looked at me from her half-lowered eyes, while the smoke drifted between us.

"Beautiful," I said. "I've practiced that look for hours in my mirror and I can't seem to get it like that."

"Bastard," she said, and straightened up. "If I faint will you blow into my mouth?"

"No," I said. I treated myself to one of my cigarettes.

"Well," Mousy said, "you are different. Did you know Linda's first husband?"

"Yes."

"Boring man. Took himself so unutterably seriously. Do you take yourself seriously?"

"Thursdays," I said, "when I go for my pedicure."

Mousy smiled and took a significant guzzle of her martini. She reached out with her left hand and squeezed my arm.

"My," she said, "don't we have biceps."

I let that slide. All the answers I could think of sounded a little silly, including *yes* and *no*.

"Do detectives have fights, Mr. Marlowe?" she said.

"Sometimes," I said. "Usually we put the criminal in his place with a well-polished phrase."

"Are you carrying a gun?"

I shook my head. "I didn't know you'd be here," I said.

A leathery specimen with short grey hair came over and put a hand on her elbow. Her smile was all light and no heat as she turned toward him.

"Mr. Marlowe," she said, "this is my husband, Morton Fairchild."

Morton nodded at me without interest.

"Pleased," he said, and steered his wife away from the bar and toward the dance floor.

"I don't think that man liked me," I said to Tino.

"It is not that, Mr. Marlowe," Tino said. "I do not think that he wishes his wife to be near both a man and a bar."

"You don't miss much, do you, Tino?"

"No, Mr. Marlowe, only those things I am supposed to miss."

Linda appeared with a guest.

"Darling," she said, "I'd love to have you meet Cord Havoc. Cord, this is my husband, Philip Marlowe."

"By God, Marlowe, I'm glad to meet you," Havoc said. He put out a big square hand. I shook it firmly. I knew who he was all right. I'd seen him in three or four bad movies. He was a dreamboat, six feet tall, even features, a strong jaw, pale blue eyes set wide apart. His teeth were perfectly even. His clothes fit him the way Tino's tux fitted him.

"I'm damned glad, Marlowe, that this little girl has finally found the right guy. Broke my heart and a lot of others when she did, but damn it's good to see her happy."

I smiled at him becomingly. While I was smiling he held his glass out toward Tino without even looking at him and Tino filled it with bourbon. Havoc took a good third of it at a swallow.

"Cord's new picture will be opening next week," Linda said.

"Gangster show," Havoc said, and took in another third of his drink. "Probably seem pretty tame to you, Marlowe."

"Sure would," I said. "Normally this time of the afternoon I strangle an alligator."

Havoc put his head back and laughed loudly. Then he finished his drink.

"Atta boy, Phil." He held his now empty glass out and Tino hit it again. "You can thank me, boy. All the time before she met you I was looking out for her." He laughed again, with the tossing head movement that he'd used before.

"Cord, you know you weren't looking out for me," Linda said. "You were attempting to get me into bed."

Cord's muzzle was in his drink. He took it out and gave me a little elbow and said, "Can you blame me, Phil?"

As he spoke his eyes swept the room. He was not a boy who wanted to miss a chance. Before I had a chance to say whether I blamed him, he spotted someone.

"Hey, Manny," he shouted and burst off across the dining room toward a weasly-looking little bald guy with a deep tan and an open shirt, with the collar carefully out over the lapels of his cream and plaid camel jacket.

"Must have been hard," I said to Linda, "not to tumble in the hay with him."

"Mostly," Linda said, "when he tumbles into the hay, he passes out."

She leaned over and kissed me lightly on the lips.

"Right out in public?" I said.

"I want everyone to know who belongs to whom, here," she said.

"Mostly it matters that you and I know," I said.

She smiled and patted my cheek. "We do, darling, don't we."

I nodded and she swept off to greet a new guest as if they had risen from the dead. Mousy Fairchild seemed to have shaken off her husband for a moment and swept past me with a tall dark guy in a good suit. She stopped, ordered another martini from Tino and said, "Meet the lucky man," to the dark guy in the good suit.

"Mr. Marlowe," she said to me, "this is Mr. Steele."

Steele put out his hand. His eyes were steady and blank, his face was healthy looking and smooth. He was a man who looked like he could move quickly and you better move quickly too. We shook hands. Mousy's husband trudged over and retrieved her.

I said, "Used to be a guy named Steele, Arnie Steele, ran the rackets in San Berdoo and Riverside."

"Is that so?" Steele said. "Understand you're a private cop."

"When I'm not passing canapes," I said, "and cleaning up after bridge parties."

"Nice little deal," Steele said, "marrying into all that dough."

"Peachy," I said. "I heard this Steele guy got out of the rackets, maybe four, five years ago. Bought himself a place in the desert."

"Knew when to get out, huh?" Steele said.

"Uh huh," I said.

The weasly little bald guy with the deep tan and the open shirt came over to Steele.

"Arnie," he said, "excuse me, but I'd like you to meet

somebody. Cord Havoc, the movie star, biggest thing in the country this year. We're thinking of putting something together you might be interested in."

Steele nodded without expression as the weasel edged him away from me with his shoulder. As he left Steele glanced at me over the weasel's head.

"Stay loose, Shoo-Fly," he said.

I nodded. Tino stepped over and refreshed my drink with a lovely little economical flourish. When I turned back from the bar I was nose to nose and elsewhere with a piece of blond business in a frantic décolletage who was drunker than two billy goats. Her eyes were very large and very blue.

"Are you in pictures, Mr. Marlowe?"

"I couldn't make it," I said. "They went for the horse instead."

"Somebody said you was in pictursh," she said. The s's were all slushy. She leaned against me and the push-'em-up underwire bra jammed into my rib cage.

"I'm in pictures," she said.

"I knew you were," I said.

"I'm an actress." The s's were increasingly difficult for her. "I'm in a lot of pirate things. I play a wench. You know? I wear low dresses and bend over in front of the camera a lot. Director says to me do your dip, now, Cherry. Like everybody knows about me."

"Now I do too," I said. She was not leaning into me out of passion, she was leaning for support.

"Did you come with someone?" I said.

"Sure, Mr. Steele brought me. I'd never come to some swell's house like this, unless Mr. Steele or somebody brought me."

"Aw, I bet you get to go everywhere," I said.

She smiled at me and hiccupped and began to slide to the floor. I got her under the arms and dragged her back upright, got my left arm around her back and my right under her knees and hoisted her up in my arms just as all strength left her and she went limp.

Tino came around the bar.

"Sir?"

"Tell Mr. Steele I'd like to see him, Tino."

Tino nodded and glided across the room, moving through the crowd without any apparent effort, bumping into no one. I saw him speak to Steele, who turned and glanced at me. His face didn't change but he nodded once, looked at the front door and jerked his head toward me.

A languid blond man with longish hair reassembled himself away from the wall where he'd been leaning and came over to me.

"I'll take her," he said.

"She's dead weight," I said. "Can you handle her?"

He grinned and put out his arms. I transferred her and he ambled away, out the front door and into the darkness. In maybe two minutes he was back.

"In the car," he said, "back seat, on her side. Lay her on her back and she snores."

"Thanks," I said. He nodded and went back to his post by the front door. Steele never glanced at him or me again.

"The lady is all right, Mr. Marlowe?"

"Sleeping it off in the car, Tino."

"The lady may be more fortunate than you, sir."

"Think of the excitement she's missing," I said.

"Yes, sir," Tino said.

12

I was on the road early, before the heat got hard, heading west to Los Angeles. Marlowe the commuting gumshoe. Works in L.A., lives in Poodle Springs. Spends 20 hours a day on the road.

The desert was empty this early, except for tumbleweed, cactus and an occasional hawk riding the wind currents with an eye out for breakfast. I passed a place that sold date shakes. Hard to imagine a date shake. My only company into L.A. were the big ten wheelers that passed you with a rush of air on the downgrades and blocked you on the upgrades as they downshifted.

The sky was high and bright when I got to L.A. I

got off the freeway at Spring Street and parked. Inside City Hall near the City Clerk's Office was a small room under the big central stairway. On the grimy pebbled glass door, lettered in black, was *OFFICE OF THE PARKING CLERK.* I went in. Across the front of the room was a long counter, behind a railing were three elderly female clerks, to the right behind a railing were three small hearing cubicles. There was a line for each. I got in line for the counter. The line shuffled slowly forward, old people in worn clothing paying parking fines with postal money orders, sharp guys in flashy suits paying in cash and trying to look like this was just a minor annoyance, interrupting a day of important conferences. The clerk running my line was very fat, so that her head seemed to rest on her shoulders and her chins merged with her breastbone. Her hair was white with a pronounced blue tone, and she wheezed a little as she processed the tickets, very slowly.

When I reached her she said, "Present the ticket, cash? check? or money order?"

I smiled at her like a man about to propose marriage.

"Perhaps you can help me," I said.

She didn't look up. "Not unless you present your ticket."

I slid a piece of paper over the counter to her. I had

written the number of Les Valentine's L.A. parking ticket on it.

"I wonder if you could tell me where that violation occurred," I said.

"You got a complaint, or wish to contest, step behind that railing and wait for the hearing officer."

"I have no complaint," I said. "I'm trying to locate the address where this ticket was issued. I'm trying to locate a missing person."

In the line behind me people were beginning to mutter.

The woman looked up at me. She had small eyes and a little hooked nose like a chicken.

"You want to pay a ticket or not," she said. "There's people waiting."

"That's it," I said, "two choices?"

"You trying to be smart with me, Buster?" she said.

"Hell, no," I said. "Be a waste of time."

I turned and pushed through the crowd and out the door. In an angle near the front door was a bank of pay phones. I got one, put in my coin and called the office of the parking clerk. An elderly female voice answered.

"Yeah," I said. "This is Marlowe, Sheriff's Sub Station in Encino. I need a location on a parking ticket."

"We're busy," the elderly female voice said. "Put it through on a requisition form."

"Listen, Sis," I snarled, "you think you're talking to some biscuit kicker from Fresno? This is police business, so get off your widest part and get me an address."

There was a sharp intake of breath on the other end and then the voice said, "What's the number on the violation?"

I read her the ticket number and said, "Hubba hubba, Sis. I don't have all day."

The line was silent for a few minutes and then she was back on, very distant. "The violation occurred in front of 1254 Western Avenue," she said. "And I must say I don't appreciate your manner."

I said, "Whyn't you go kiss a walrus, Sis," and hung up.

1254 Western Avenue was on the west side of the block between Hollywood and Sunset boulevards, next to a taco stand. It was a three-story building of the kind they built out there right after the war, before they knew that Hollywood would turn into a sleaze bucket and they thought they were at the avant edge of modern architecture. It was square and full of glass that needed to be washed. The facing was some kind of brushed aluminum in big squares, so that the place looked like an ugly bread box fallen on hard times. On the first floor, behind a plate-glass window, was an office that sold real estate and insurance. An old guy who looked like he might be brother to the lady at the parking clerk's office was sitting in his shirtsleeves bent over an old-fashioned ledger. A redhead who would look like the parking clerk's sister in maybe ten years was sitting at her desk doing her nails.

The entry hall was to the left of the real estate office and a stairway led up along the left wall. There was no elevator. On the wall beside the door to the real estate office was a directory, one of those black felt numbers with slots where white letters were inserted. The glass that covered it was flyspecked and stained with years of smog. There was no Les Valentine listed. Of the ten tenants on three floors, there was one photographer. *Larry Victor,* it said, *Photoportraits.* Same initials, I thought. Why not?

I went up two flights. The building smelled as if cats lived in the stairwells. Larry Victor was on the third floor, at the back. There was some light showing through the pebbled glass on his door. It had the white look of daylight, as if there were a window opposite, or a skylight. The lettering said *Larry Victor, Photographer, Advertising, Industrial. Portraits a Specialty.* I knocked; no answer. I tried the knob; locked. I didn't have my collection of passkeys, but I did carry in my inside pocket a tool I'd taken from a safe and loft guy once. It looked something like one of those dental tools that technicians use to scrape your teeth. Only the needle nose was longer. I edged the nose inside the jamb overlap and turned it so that it put pressure on the lock tongue. It was a spring type and popped right back. I was in. I closed the door behind me and looked around.

The place looked like the kind of office I'd spent half my life in. An old rolltop desk, a wobbly swivel chair with a worn pillow on the seat, an oak filing cabinet, and against one wall a big sheet of white paper taped up, and a couple of still cameras on tripods and some photographer's lamps grouped in front of it. I looked at the cameras. There was a Rolleiflex on one tripod and a Canon 35 mm on the other. The daylight poured in through a dirty skylight webbed with chicken wire. There was a phone on the desk and an onyx pen and pencil set.

I went around and sat in the swivel chair. It didn't have to be this building, of course. The car could have been parked here and Valentine could have gone up to Hollywood Boulevard looking for movie stars. Or down to Sunset looking for excitement. Or he could have caught a cab to Bakersfield where he had about as much chance for either.

Still, the car was tagged outside this building and here was a photographer with the same initials. I inventoried the desk. On top was a picture of a pretty black-haired woman, maybe 25, with big dark eyes. The cubbyholes were stuffed mostly with bills, a lot of them unpaid, including three more traffic tickets. The middle drawer had a Greater L.A. street map, the lower left drawer held L.A. phone directories, the lower right drawer had a bottle of cheap Scotch with maybe five ounces gone. I got up and went across to the file cabinet. The top drawer contained a car insurance policy, an unopened bottle of the same Scotch, a package of paper cups and a big manila envelope with a small metal clasp at the top. I opened the envelope. In it was a collection of 8 × 10 glossy prints of naked women doing a variety of tricks, some of them quite old. The other two file drawers were empty.

I took the big envelope over to the desk and sat back down and began to look a little more carefully at what there was. What there was was porn, a lot of it, pretty good quality, some of it maybe shot in front of the very white paper backdrop that stood to my right. It had been quite some time since pictures of people copulating had stimulated my libido, and this stuff was no different. Even if it had been stimulating it was so much that overkill would have suffocated randiness in the simple mass of overindulgence that it represented.

In addition to being pretty well lit, and in good focus, the pictures were of generally attractive models. Actresses no doubt, come to Hollywood, soon to be stars, or maybe starlets, waiting for the right part. The men in the pictures were props for the women, obscure, generally faceless, no more noticeable than the lamp in the background, or the bare metal leg of the daybed on which the action took place.

I flipped through the pictures and stopped. There, looking younger, as naked as she had been only a few days earlier, was Sondra Lee, posing alone, suggestively, with the same empty-eyed smile. I slipped it out of the pack, rolled it the short way, put a rubber band around it and slipped it into my inside coat pocket. I riffled through the rest of the pictures without encountering anyone else I knew and got up and put the folder back into the file drawer. I went back and sat down in the swivel and put my feet up and thought about it a little. The coincidences were piling up, photographer, same initials, picture of Sondra Lee.

While I was thinking about these things, I heard a key scratch on the lock, then go into the keyhole. There was no place to hide. So I kept sitting, with my feet up. The key turned, the door opened and in came a guy who looked like a finalist in the Mr. Southern California pageant. He had longish blond hair, combed straight back. His face was tanned, he was slim, medium height, medium build. He wore a cream sport coat and white pants, and a black shirt with a big collar that spilled out over his lapels.

When he saw me, he stopped, pulled his head back an inch, raised his eyebrows and stared at me.

"Don't be confused," I said. "I am not you."

"I can see that, Chappy," he said, "but who the hell are you?"

"You first," I said.

"Me first? This is my office."

"Ah ha," I said. "You must be Larry Victor."

"Yes, I must," he said. "But I still don't know you. Or why you're sitting in my chair, or how you got in."

"Kind of like a nursery rhyme, isn't it?" I said.

Victor stood with the door still open, in case he needed to run.

"Are you going to tell me?" he said.

"Marlowe," I said. "I'm looking for a guy named Les Valentine."

"You a cop?"

"Nope," I said. "I met Valentine at a card game, I stayed pat with two pair. He had a flush. He took my marker for half a g and gave me this address."

"And the door?" Victor said. "I suppose it was open?"

"Yeah," I said, "as a matter of fact it was."

Victor nodded. "Mind if I sit at my desk, Marlowe?"

I stood, stepped aside, and he sat.

"I think I'll have a short one," Victor said, "Join me?"

"Sure," I said. He rummaged the cheap Scotch out of the drawer and poured some into a couple of paper cups. I had a swallow. It tasted like something you'd take for mange. Victor guzzled it down and poured another couple of inches into the paper cup. Then he leaned back in his swivel and tried to look easy. While he was looking easy he edged a glance at the file cabinet. Then he looked back at me.

"Funny thing," Victor said. "I know Les Valentine."

"Amazing," I said.

"Not so amazing, really. We're both in the same line. Both do a lot of movie still work, publicity stuff, that sort of thing. Do a lot of high-fashion stuff too."

I glanced around the office.

"Hey," he said, "don't waste money on fancy front stuff, you understand? You got the goods, you don't need all that floss and gloss stuff, you know, all that Hollywood flash."

"I can see that you're not wasting time on that," I said. I swished a little more of his Scotch around in my mouth. If I was going to drink it I might as well try to prevent cavities while I was at it. Victor didn't seem to be having any problem with it. He was already pouring out a third slug. Maybe he was tougher than he looked.

"So I know Les, like I was saying. Good photographer."

"Where is he now?" I said.

"I heard he was out of the country," Victor said.

I believed that like I believed I was drinking Chivas Regal.

"Some kind of work for the government. China, I think."

He leaned back and savored his drink, just a breezy guy, passing the time, having a drink with a guy who'd broken into his office. He was as authentic as a starlet's smile.

"Know a model named Sondra Lee?" I said.

"Sonny? Of course, any photographer would know Sonny. She's the top model on the coast."

"Ever photograph her?"

"Naw, never had the pleasure myself. I mean, I've been approached, but you know how it is, Marlowe. You got commitments, she's got commitments. We've never been able to get together."

"Even when she was younger?" I said. I had no idea where I was going. I just wanted to keep it going. Something might surface.

He shook his head. "When she was young, pal, I wasn't in the business. Sonny's no coed, you know."

I nodded, and eased another small sip of the Scotch into my mouth, sort of sneaking around on it from the side. It was still putrid.

"How about Manny Lipshultz?" I said.

If it hit him oddly he didn't show anything. He pursed his lips slightly and looked up at the corner of the room. Then he shook his head.

"Nope, no Manny Lipshultz," he said. "Swell name though, ain't it."

I agreed that it was swell. We were all swell. He and I were especially swell, just a couple of swell guys sitting around lying to each other on a pleasant afternoon.

13

I went out onto Western Avenue and sat in my car and waited. While I waited I tried to figure out what I thought I was doing. I knew I was getting ready to tail a guy who wasn't the man I was looking for, but he had a picture of Sondra Lee and an office in a building where the guy I was looking for had gotten a ticket. There was no reason to do it except the guy was all wrong. You walk into your office and find a guy there you don't sit down and drink with him. You call the buttons.

About twenty minutes after I started sitting and waiting, Victor came out of his office building and headed down Western on foot. I waited until he got to the corner, and when he turned right on Sunset I got out of the Olds and hot-footed it after him, slowing to a casual walk when I reached Sunset. I crossed to the south side of Sunset and headed west. Victor was across the street from me, maybe fifty yards ahead. He had a furtive quality to his walk, but it was probably instinctive. He didn't look around. Halfway down the next block he turned into a bar called Reno's. I let him settle in, then I sidled in myself and slid into a booth near the front. The waitress scowled at me, one guy in a booth for four.

"I'm part of the Southern Cal backfield," I said. "My teammates will be joining me soon."

"Everybody's funny as hell, out here," she said. "You want a drink?"

I ordered a gimlet, on the rocks, and sipped it slowly, letting it work against the taste of Victor's deadly Scotch. Victor was at the bar, on a stool, shoulders hunched over a shot of something which, judging from his Scotch, probably tasted like an old pipe cleaner.

Beside him was a blonde in a very short skirt, her legs crossed, sitting sideways on the bar stool, leaning toward Victor. She had on green eye shadow and very bright red lipstick, and her green and red tank top gaped a little at the back of her skirt as she leaned forward. The only other person at the bar was an aging redhead with a big chest confined by a white sequined sweater that was raveled at the sleeve. She was drinking Manhattans, and while I watched, the bartender brought her one and gestured toward Larry Victor. She took it, nodded her thanks at Victor and dipped into it. Larry made a little salute back at her with two fingers touching his forehead and turned his attention to La Blondie.

La Blondie was demanding it. I couldn't hear her, but from the intensity of her movements and the speed with which her mouth moved it was clear that she was mad as hell. Victor kept shaking his head and muttering back at her.

The inside of Reno's was fake knotty pine, with a few longhorns mounted on the wall, and some old Frederic Remington prints framed here and there around the room. It was not very bright inside, and the brightness of the Southern California sun outside made it seem even dimmer. It was cool, and would probably have been quiet if the redhead at the end hadn't kept feeding the jukebox. A cool bar on a hot afternoon is a very comfortable place sometimes.

The blonde took something that looked like a photo from her purse and shoved it toward him. Victor took a pair of rimless glasses from the breast pocket of his shapeless sport coat and put them on to look at the picture. When he saw the picture he quickly put his hand over it, palm flat, and looked around the room, uncomfortably. Then he shoved the picture back at the blonde, took his glasses off and put them away. The blonde picked up the photograph and put it back in her purse. The whole exchange probably hadn't lasted more than twenty seconds, but it had been enough, when he had looked around the bar with his rimless glasses on, for me to realize what bothered me about him. Except for the hair, he looked like the picture I'd seen of Les Valentine. And hair can be arranged.

Victor stood up suddenly, slammed a ten on the bar and walked out of the bar like a man leaving his wife for good. The blonde sat staring after him. I got up and went after Victor, being careful not to step into the blonde's gaze. It would have punched holes in my rib cage.

He was halfway to the corner of Western when I came out of the bar. By the time he got his car from the curb near his office I was in my Olds with the motor idling. He went west on Sunset until he hit the freeway and south to Venice Boulevard. It was the middle of a bright afternoon and traffic was easy. I kept two or three cars between me and Victor, and shifted lanes from time to time. He wasn't expecting to be tailed, and he had other things on his mind. I could have followed him in a ferris wheel.

I followed him down to the beach. And when he pulled into the narrow parking slot behind a beach-front bungalow, I went on past and parked under an olive tree between two trash barrels under a sign that said *Private Parking, This Means You.* I walked back to the beach bungalow, past the backs of dank little clap-board houses, each with a car rammed up against its back wall, squeezed in off the street. Once, someone had planted olive trees along this road, and here and there where the salt wind hadn't killed them they grew stunted and misshapen, littering the ground with in-complete black olives that looked like human drop-pings. The harsh smell of their leaves mingled with the sea smell and the scent of cooking, and under it the rich evasive smell of decaying garbage from the over-filled trash cans that shared the tiny back space with the cars.

Behind Victor's house, at the little cement pad path that led around the house to the front door, was a mail-box. The lettering on it said *Larry and Angel Victor.* I went on, two houses down, and cut through another narrow cement pad path with weeds forcing up through the sand beneath the pads. In front of the houses was the beach walk and then the beach and then the fat Pacific Ocean waddling in onto the coastline.

Two houses down, Larry Victor was sitting on a

beach chair on his front porch with his feet up on the railing. Next to him was the black-haired young woman with big dark eyes from the picture on his desk. She had on some kind of loose-fitting Hawaiian dress and little white sling strap high-heeled shoes, and she had let the dress slide halfway up her thighs as she sat with her feet up beside Victor's. They were drinking Mexican beer from the bottle and holding hands. It was the kind of domestic scene that the insurance companies use when they try to tell you that enough life insurance will make you secure. I stood halfway behind a patch of giant geraniums, at the corner of the beach house two doors down, and watched.

Marlowe, the all-seeing, sees all, peeps at everything. The girl leaned over and kissed Victor and the kiss lingered and developed. When the kiss and ensuing struggle ended Victor reached up in an automatic gesture and straightened his hair. I smiled. Bingo. Les Valentine with a hairpiece.

14

I drove back to the Springs in time for a late supper which Tino made up for me in the kitchen. Linda was at the Racquet Club and didn't get home until I was finishing the last of the salad that Tino insisted on serving after the meal.

"It is how it is done, Mr. Marlowe," Tino said. "Everyone does it this way in the Springs."

"Everybody but me, Tino," I said. "I eat my salad before the meal."

Tino shook his head. "Mrs. Marlowe said we will never civilize you, Mr. Marlowe."

"I'm as civilized as I'm likely to get," I said.

"You are very fine the way you are, Mr. Marlowe."

At which point Linda entered.

"Well, darling," she said, "look at you home from a hard day's gumshoeing. How nice."

She came over and gave me a light kiss. I could smell the booze on her breath.

"Would you like some supper too, Mrs. Marlowe?"

"No, Tino, please, just a large Scotch, light soda, on the rocks."

Linda sat across from me in the kitchen. Tino brought her the drink.

"Did you detect anything very good today, darling?"

"I found Les Valentine," I said.

"How exciting for you. I'm sure it compensates for missing our dinner at the club with Mousy and Morton."

"Perfect," I said. "Myrna Loy couldn't have read it better."

"Don't be rude, darling. You did stand me up, you know."

"I know," I said. "And I'm sorry I had to. But the whistle doesn't blow at cocktail time, for me."

"And I knew that when I married you," Linda said.

There was nothing in that for me. I let it pass.

"It would be encouraging, darling, if sometimes I felt that you'd shirk the job to be with me."

"It is the only way I can be with you," I said. "Your

old man has about a hundred million bucks. If I start shirking my job to be with you, pretty soon I'll be laying around having my eyebrows plucked."

"You're such a goddamned fool," Linda said.

"Probably," I said.

Linda nuzzled her drink again.

"Don't you even want to be with me?" she said.

"Damn it, that's the point. Of course I want to be with you. I'd like to spend all my time in bed with you, having cocktails by the pool with you, helping you sort your lingerie. And if I give in to that, what am I? You could get me a little jeweled collar and we could go for walks."

Linda stood and turned away from me, the drink half finished in her hand. She took two steps toward the door, stopped, threw the glass at the sink. It missed and banged against the cabinet and broke and splattered on the rug. She turned and collapsed into my lap with her mouth against mine.

"You bastard," she said, her mouth open against mine. "You unbreakable bastard."

I picked her up and headed for the bedroom. Money had its uses. Tino would clean up the drink.

In the morning Linda had a headache and we stayed in bed drinking orange juice and coffee and waiting for the headache to dwindle.

"Too much Scotch," I said.

"Of course not," Linda said. "I go to a quiet party and have a couple of teenie drinks, and come home sleepy, and . . . well, I certainly didn't get much sleep."

"I noticed that," I said.

Tino rapped softly on the bedroom door and then came in with a breakfast tray.

She turned her head away quite quickly.

"Ah, but Mrs. Marlowe," Tino said with a smile. "Mr. Marlowe will eat his and most of yours, I believe."

Tino put the tray down on my side of the bed and went out. I set to work to prove him right.

"How can you, you beast," Linda said.

"Exercise," I said. "Healthy indoor exercise all night. Makes me hungry."

Without looking, Linda groped over, found half a piece of toast and took a small bite of the point. She chewed it carefully. Then she leaned back against the pillow carefully to rest and let it settle.

"You said last night that you found Muffy Blackstone's husband," Linda said softly, her eyes still closed.

"Yes," I said. "He's living in Venice under the name Larry Victor. Has a photography studio in Hollywood."

"I'm sure Mr. Lipshultz will be very proud of you, darling."

"If I tell him."

"Why wouldn't you?" Linda said.

I was looking at her profile, the way the fine vein pulsed in her lowered eyelids.

"There appears to be a Mrs. Victor."

Linda rolled her head over on the pillow so she was full face to me and slowly opened both eyes.

"Is there really," she said. "That little, timid, water bug of a man?"

"In L.A. he wears a rug and no glasses. A regular stallion."

"A rug?"

"A toupee, long blond, smoothed back," I said. "Dresses like the agent for a B-picture starlet." I reached over to my bed table and got the rolled-up picture of Sondra Lee. I handed it to Linda.

"He specializes in this type of picture," I said.

Linda looked at the photograph and turned it quickly over in her lap.

"Oh," Linda said. Then she turned the picture back over carefully and peeked at it again. Her eyebrows came together in the loveliest frown I'd ever seen. She studied the photograph again.

"Her breasts are awfully small," Linda said, "and she has a little pot belly."

"That's hardly a pot belly," I said.

"Men like pictures like this?"

"Some men," I said.

She looked at me, and silently pulled the covers back.

"I like the real thing," I said.

She nodded her head slowly, as if satisfied with the answer, and put the covers over her again.

"Muffy's husband takes pictures like this?"

"Hundreds," I said.

"How did you find them?" Linda said.

"I burgled his office," I said. "Don't tell."

She wrinkled her nose.

"Must you do this work?" she said.

I didn't answer. She put her hand on my arm.

"Yes," she said, "of course you must. It's just so . . ."

"Yeah," I said. "Isn't it."

We were quiet for a moment. Linda studied the picture some more.

"So why don't you tell Mr. Lipshultz?"

"I don't know. It's just that, he and the other wife . . . I followed him home. She was glad to see him . . ." I shrugged.

"Well, what about Muffy?" Linda said.

"Yeah," I said.

"Oh," Linda said.

She looked once more at the picture. Then she put

it down on her night table and turned toward me and paused. She rolled back onto her back, reached over and turned the picture facedown, then turned back to me.

"I'm feeling ever so much better," she said.

15

I was beginning to feel like a pinball, bouncing back and forth between Poodle Springs and L.A. I came in through the Valley this time and drove in on Cahuenga. Hollywood Boulevard looked like it always did in the morning, like a hooker with her make-up off.

I parked on Hollywood near Wilton and walked back to Western. I had Sondra Lee's picture in my pocket. It was time to talk with Larry/Les.

The old fat geezer was still at his desk in the real estate office when I went in. The stairs still smelled of old dampness and sour lives as I went up. Victor's office door was unlocked and I went in. He wasn't there, but something was.

She was in his swivel chair, tilted back, her head back, her arms hanging stiffly down. There was a small hole in the middle of her forehead with the flesh around it puffy a little and discolored. I couldn't see the blood, but I could smell it. Dried, probably, in a black stain on the floor behind her. Her mouth was open and her stiffened lips were curved with the harsh rictus smile I'd seen too often.

I could feel my stomach clench. Under the dried blood smell I could still detect the lingering odor of cordite. I closed the office door behind me and walked closer and looked down at the dead woman's face. I'd seen it before but it took me a minute to place where. She was the blonde who had argued with Larry Victor in Reno's café. I touched her cheek. The skin was cold. I moved one of her arms. It was stiff. There was a puddle of dried blood on the floor behind her chair.

I knew what I would have to do eventually, but first I went to the file cabinet and opened it. The pictures were gone. I looked over the rest of the office. Nothing else seemed to be missing. I looked again at the blonde's dead face. Took in a deep breath, and dialed the cops.

The first to arrive were a couple of deputies from the West Hollywood sheriff's station on San Vicente. They came in wearing the usual wary expressions behind the usual sunglasses. One of them knelt to check the body, the other one talked to me.

"You touch anything?" he said. His voice was hard.

"The phone," I said.

"How come?" in a voice that sounded like I'd better have a good reason.

"To call you," I said.

He nodded. The other one stood up. "Been dead awhile," he said.

The first one grunted. "What's your story?" he said to me.

"I'm a private cop," I said. "I came here to see Larry Victor."

"A PI? How 'bout that, Harry. Are we lucky? We get a squeal and there's a PI at the other end."

"Lucky," Harry said.

"What did you come to see Victor about?" the first cop said.

"Case I'm working on," I said.

"You got some ID?"

"Sure," I said. I got out my wallet and showed him. The address on my license was still my old one in L.A.

"What's the case?" Harry said.

I shook my head. "No point to that," I said. "I'll have to go through it for the detectives. Why make me go through it twice?"

"You'll go through it as many times as we think you should, shoo-fly," the first cop said. "What's the case you're on?"

"Right now there's nothing here that tells me my case has anything to do with your case. If it does, then I'll have to tell you. But right now, I don't."

"Listen, Smart Guy," the first cop said. "You don't decide what's related to our case. We do."

"We?" I said. "You guys are baby-sitters. As soon as homicide shows up you'll be out in the black and white logging meter violations."

"Okay, Big Mouth," Harry said, "hands behind the back."

At which point Bernie Ohls came in smoking one of his toy cigars and looking like a man who had breakfasted well, and got plenty of exercise. He was the D.A.'s chief investigator.

"Annoying the prowl car boys again, Marlowe?" he said.

The two Sheriff's Deputies didn't exactly stand to attention, but they straightened up visibly. Harry stopped with the handcuffs half off his belt.

"Ohls," Bernie said. "D.A.'s office."

"Yes, sir, Lieutenant, we know," the first cop said.

Bernie smiled without any meaning and nodded toward the door. "We've got it now," he said, and the two deputies went out of the office. Ohls walked over and looked down at the dead woman. He was a medium-sized guy with blond hair and stiff white eyebrows. His teeth were even and white and his pale blue eyes were very calm. He spoke in a pleasant, cop-smart voice that was always a hair too casual to trust. There were two other county employees with him, both in plain clothes. They didn't pay any attention to me at all.

"Close up," Ohls said as he looked down at the body, "small-caliber gun, probably hot-loaded, made a much bigger hole going out, I'd say, than going in."

One of the county employees said, "M.E. will be here in a minute, Lieutenant."

Ohls nodded absently. "Know her?" he said to me.

"No," I said.

Ohls looked up and hard at me. "You being cute?" he said.

"Not yet," I said.

He nodded again. The M.E. appeared, a short fat guy wearing a suit and a vest, with a large cigar tucked into the right corner of his mouth. Two lab guys came in behind him and began to dust for fingerprints.

"Come on," Ohls said to me and we went out into the tight hallway.

"Tell me your story," Ohls said. He took in a little cigar smoke and let it out softly in the dim hallway.

"Missing person job out of the Springs," I said. "Trail led here. I talked to the guy in the office, he said he couldn't help me. Said he knew my guy, but my guy was off somewhere and wasn't coming back. I went away, looked around some more, found some things that didn't make sense and came back to talk to this guy again. The door was open. I walked in and found her."

"Guy's name Larry Victor?" Ohls said.

"That's the name on the door," I said.

"You know where he is now?"

"No," I said.

"Anything else you can tell me, might help?" Ohls said.

"No."

"I suppose if I asked you the name of your client you wouldn't tell me," Ohls said.

"Guy in my line, Bernie, doesn't get ahead telling the cops who he's working for if he doesn't have to," I said.

"And who decides if he has to?" Ohls said.

I shrugged. "We work it out," I said.

"Sure we do," Ohls said. He took the toy cigar out of his mouth and looked at it quietly for a moment, then dropped it on the floor and ground it out with his foot.

"Stay in touch," Ohls said and turned and went back into the office. I looked after him for a minute and couldn't see any space in there for me. So I left.

16

I went down Western and west on Santa Monica Boulevard with my foot heavy on the gas pedal. It wouldn't
take the buttons very long to find out where Larry Victor lived, and then somebody would cruise down there
and pick him up. I wanted to get there first, and I wasn't
sure exactly why. I made it to Venice Beach in 25 minutes and my right leg was a little shaky when I finally
took it off the gas pedal and climbed out of the Olds behind Victor's beachfront house. There was no squad car
in sight. I went around in front of the beach house and
in through the patio and knocked on the sliding glass
door. The dark-haired young woman I'd seen with Victor before came to the door and slid it a short way open.

"Yes?"

"Marlowe," I said. "I need to see Larry Victor quick."

She smiled and slid the door wider.

"Come in, Mr. Marlowe," she said. "Larry's fixing us drinks in the kitchen. Would you like one?"

"In a minute we'll all need one," I said. "Tell Larry it's urgent."

As I spoke Victor came out of the kitchen with a pitcher and two glasses. He looked at me.

"What the hell do you want?" he said.

"I can't take time to explain," I said. "You'll have to take my word. There's a dead woman in your office, Victor, and the cops are on the way."

Angel's eyes widened. Victor said, "A dead woman?"

I said, "Come on, get in my car. Angel, tell the cops you don't know where he is." Everyone stood stock still. I took Victor's arm.

"It's me or a long night downtown," I said. "Angel, dump the glass and drinks. We'll be back."

I pulled Victor with me and went out the front door.

"Larry," Angel yelled after us, "call me."

"Get rid of the two glasses," I said. Then I had Victor in my car and we were rolling out onto Lincoln Ave and onto Venice Boulevard, heading east.

"What the hell is this, Marlowe?" Victor said. I offered him a cigarette. He took it and lit it from the lighter in my dashboard. The car filled with the smell that cigarettes only smell like when you light them with a car lighter.

He took in a deep inhale and let it out in two streams through his nostrils.

"Okay," he said, "what's going on?"

I told him, all of it.

"I didn't kill her," Victor said. "I don't even know what she was doing in my office."

"But you knew her," I said.

"The hell you say."

"She was the blonde you had a fight with the other day in Reno's Bar," I said.

Victor stared at me for a moment. His mouth opened and closed like a tropical fish.

"How'd you . . ." he said and let it hang.

"I followed you," I said.

"Followed me?"

"Try not to say everything I say. I followed you to Reno's, and then I followed you home. Is Angel your wife?"

"Yes," he said.

"And is Muriel Valentine your wife?"

"Muriel Valentine?"

"I told you not to do that," I said.

"Who's Muriel Valentine?"

"Les Valentine's wife," I said. "I saw a picture of him in her house. If you put on your glasses and took off your rug you'd look just like him."

He was silent for a moment, while he sucked on his cigarette. A long red coal began to form on the end, the way it does when several people pass one around. He shook his head and opened the window of my car and threw the glowing snipe out onto the pavement. A few sparks shook loose as we drove away from it. I could feel his stare.

"So what's the deal?" he said. His voice was heavy.

"Do I call you Larry or Les?" I said.

He didn't answer.

"You legally married to Angel?"

He still didn't answer.

"This is certainly pleasant," I said, "talking to myself. No smart guy remarks, no lies, just the soothing sound of my own questions." I got the picture of Sondra Lee out of my inside pocket and slipped the band off and unrolled it with one hand while I drove. It was nothing compared to brain surgery.

"I assume when you took this she was just starting out," I said. I handed the picture to him. He took it, still silent. Then he said, "Jesus Christ, Marlowe."

"So tell me about things," I said.

Again he said, "Jesus Christ."

"Things fall apart," I said. "Murder does that. You have it all rolled up and folded away neat and then there's a murder and everything unravels."

"What am I going to do?" Larry said.

"You're going to tell me what's going on," I said. "Maybe I can work something out."

"The cops know about me?" he said.

"Not from me," I said. "When I left them they just had the corpse in your office."

"You were there?"

"I discovered the body."

We were heading north now, on Sepulveda.

"You?"

"Stiff-a-minute Marlowe," I said. "I went there to talk with you about being Larry Victor and Les Valentine. I'll call you Larry around here. Door was open, she was there. In your chair. Somebody had shot her from close up with a small-caliber gun."

"And you took that picture from my files?"

"No, I took it last time I was there. This time your files were empty."

"No pictures?"

"No pictures," I said.

"Got another cigarette?" he said.

I handed him the pack. On the right was a Von's

Supermarket. The lot was full of station wagons and women and market carriages. I pulled off Sepulveda and parked in among them.

Victor had a cigarette going. He handed me back the pack and I put it on the dashboard.

"What's your racket, Marlowe? You a grifter?"

I shook my head.

"Private License," I said. "I was hired to find you."

"Who? Muriel?"

"Lipshultz," I said.

His eyes widened. "Lippy?"

I nodded.

"For the markers?"

"Un huh."

"I was trying to build a stake," he said.

I didn't comment.

"You found out an awful lot awful fast."

"I'm a curious guy," I said. "You trying to build a stake to get out of the Springs?"

"Yeah. The Springs, Muriel, her old man, all of it."

"You married to Angel?"

"Yeah."

"Before or after Muriel?"

"Before."

"Cute," I said. "Let me guess. You met Muriel some-place, maybe shooting some pictures."

"Yeah."

"Sure," I said. "And she liked you and you saw the big burrito all of a sudden, after dancing all your life for dimes. Angel know you married her?"

"No, she thinks I go away on photography assignments."

"So you were going to get your hand in Muriel's trust fund," I said, "and when you had enough you were going to scoot back to L.A. and disappear, with Angel."

"Something like that," he said.

"Except you couldn't get the dough."

He shook his head. "Not a score," he said. "Not a bundle."

"So you tried to parlay it at the Agony Club, and found out that it's hard to beat the house."

"I gamble a lot. I'm good. I think the game was rigged."

"Sure," I said. "Otherwise you'd beat the house. I know you would. They don't play against suckers like you more than fifty, hundred times a day."

"I win a lot."

"As much as you lose?"

He didn't answer. He looked away from me at the food shoppers in the lot, busy, thinking about whether to get pot roast or lamb chops for dinner. Not thinking about a corpse in their office. Finally he spoke without looking back at me.

"So how come you didn't tell the cops?"

"What's in it for me?" I said.

"Ain't you a law-abiding citizen?"

"Within reason," I said.

"So how come you didn't tell them? How come you came tearing out here from Hollywood ahead of the cops?"

"I'm a romantic," I said.

"A what?"

"I saw you and Angel together the other night. You looked happy."

He stared at me.

"You are a piece of work, Marlowe," he said.

"Reasonably priced, too," I said.

17

The sun had moved west toward the beach and slanted in lower so that the shadows in the parking lot were long and rakish. The shopping crowd had thinned as housewives went home to start dinner and get it on the table before hubby got his third Manhattan in. The first trickle of the commuter flood was beginning to slow down on Sepulveda, heading north toward West L.A. and the Valley. Victor was browsing through my cigarettes like a goat through clover. I took the pipe out of my coat pocket and packed it and got it going right and leaned back in my seat against the door.

"I didn't kill her," Victor said.

"Say you didn't, for the moment. Say you're a shifty

bastard and a bigamist and a compulsive gambler and a pornographer and a gigolo, but say I don't see you for murder. Tell me how she ends up in your office sitting at your desk with a bullet hole in her forehead?"

"That's pretty rough, Marlowe."

"Sure it is, but it's nowhere as rough as it's going to be when you're down in the hall of justice in the back room where the cops sit around with their feet on the railing."

"If they find me," he said.

"Find you? You poor simp, I found you in three days on a skipped IOU. You think the cops can't find you on suspicion of murder one? You think I was the only person to see you argue with that blonde in Reno's? What was her name?"

"I don't know. Lola, Lola something. I hardly knew her."

"What were you arguing about?"

"She was drunk."

"What were you arguing about?"

"I used to date her," Victor said.

"Un huh, but you don't know her last name."

He shrugged. "You know how it is, Marlowe."

"No," I said. "I don't."

"You meet a lot of jillies, you sleep with them, they get to thinking it's more serious than you do."

"But not serious enough to tell you their last name," I said.

"Well, I suppose she said, but, hey, I can't remember every name, huh?" He was making a comeback, the fear was shifting back a little, into the shade. I was going to help him, oh, boy.

"Remember this one, pal, or I'll drive you straight downtown."

"Jesus Christ," he said again. The fear was back. "Don't do that. I can remember, her name was, ah . . ."

He pretended to be thinking hard.

"Her name was Faithful, Lola Faithful. I think maybe she used to hoof it a little."

"Lola Faithful," I said.

"Yeah, probably a stage name, but that's how she was in the book when I used to be dating her. Honest to God."

"And she was mad because you weren't dating her anymore."

"Yeah," Victor said, "right. She was mad as hell, Marlowe."

"How long you been married to Angel?"

"Three years and, ah, seven months."

"Break up with Lola before that?"

"Sure, hell, what kind of guy you think I am?"

"I don't want to know."

"Yeah," Victor said, "broke up with Lola long time before we got married. Soon as I started going with Angel I tossed her over."

"Uh huh," I said. "So like four years ago you ditched Lola Faithful, and a few days ago she braces you in a bar and starts screaming about it?"

"She carries a torch, Marlowe, not my fault."

I puffed a little on my pipe and squinted at him through the smoke. "I've heard sailors tell better stories to Filipino barmaids," I said.

"Well, if you don't believe me then why the hell are you sitting here with me?"

"Two things, maybe three," I said. "One, you're not the type. You're a con man, a booster, a guy that always has a little grift going, I don't think you've got the iron in your bones that it takes to kill a man."

"You ever kill anybody, tough guy?" Victor said.

"Second," I said, "why would you kill her there in your office and leave her there and not even lock the door? You'd be inviting the coppers to come and get you and say you did it."

"Yeah," he said. "I'm not that stupid."

"We'll see," I said.

"You said maybe three reasons," Victor said. "What's the other one?"

He fished the last cigarette out of my pack and

crumpled the pack and threw it out the side window. Then he pushed in the car lighter and waited for it to pop.

"Like I said, I'm a romantic."

Victor turned toward me. "I didn't kill her, Marlowe. You've got to believe that."

"I don't have to," I said. "We'll make it a working hypothesis for the moment. You got a place to coop?"

"How about your place?" Victor said.

"My place is occupied," I said.

"Yeah, but, you know, I wouldn't take up a lot of room."

"Occupied," I said, "by my wife, and myself. You're not invited."

"Christ, Marlowe, I got no place to go the cops wouldn't think of."

"They know about Muriel?" I said.

"No, Jesus, nobody knows about her."

"Go there," I said.

"Muriel's?"

"Why not? She's your wife, she thinks. It's your house."

He shook his head. "It's her house," he said. "Her and her old man's."

"You rather spend the night with your back to the wall in the lock-up?"

Victor was silent. The cigarette was down to a stub between his first two fingers. He took another drag, carefully, not burning his lips.

"How'm I going to get there?" he said.

"I'll drive you."

"All the way to Poodle Springs?"

"I live there," I said. "It's on my way home."

"You live in the Springs?" Victor said.

"Sure," I said. "Look at my jawline, the tilt of my chin."

"Marlowe," he said. "Holy Christ, are you the guy that married Harlan Potter's daughter?"

"She married me," I said.

"For chrissake, you live right down the street from me."

"Small world," I said.

18

We rode a lot of the way in silence. Victor said about every 15 minutes that he wished he had a cigarette. As we passed the Bakersfield cutoff I said, "Tell me about Muriel's father."

"Clayton Blackstone?" I could hear Victor take in air and let it out through his nose.

"Yeah."

The sun was gone now and the road cut through the empty desert like a faint ribbon in the headlights.

"Rich," Victor said.

I waited, as the highway spooled underneath us through the stationary dark.

"Rich and mean," Victor said.

"It's how you get rich," I said.

"He got rich a lot of ways," Victor said, "not all of them legal."

I waited some more.

"Most of them not legal," Victor said. "But he did it a while ago so now he's upper class and his daughter is a princess."

"It's a big rough country," I said. "Happens all the time."

"Yeah, but not to me."

"You asked for it," I said, just to be saying something.

"Blackstone made his money out of gambling, ships off the coast, out past the three-mile limit," Victor said. "Get anything you wanted out there, then. Cards, dice, roulette, a horse parlor, rooms for private games. You could get girls, booze, marijuana, coke, and this was in the days when high school kids never heard of it."

"Sure," I said, "picked you up in water taxis at the pier in Bay City."

"Now he owns banks, and hotels, and clubs and restaurants, but that's where his money came from. He's still got people around."

"Tough guys?" I said.

"Guys that'll kick out your teeth and then shoot you for mumbling."

"He connected with the Agony Club?" I said.

"Naw, Lippy runs that."

"Lippy says his boss is a guy named Blackstone, and that Blackstone is a hard number about the books."

"Jesus," Victor said, "I didn't know that." He rubbed both eyes with the heels of his open hands. "Well, old Clayton isn't going to hack me while I'm married to his daughter."

"Unless he finds out you're also married to Angel," I said.

"Jesus Christ, Marlowe."

The Poodle Springs turn-off loomed out of the night. I turned off into the deeper black of the desert roadway. There were occasional glimmers of light up the canyons where somebody had built into the slagged side of the arroyo and was squatting, doing whatever desert squatters do. I felt a million miles from anywhere, no closer to civilization than to the stars that glimmered without warmth above me. Alone in the darkness listening to the whining litany of a weak man who'd tried to be too cute.

"How do you get along with Blackstone?" I said.

"You don't get along with a guy like Blackstone,"

Victor said. "He tolerates you or he doesn't. Me he tolerates because I belong to little Muffy."

I could hear the sound of bitterness that tinged his words like the bite of an underripe orange.

"Here's how it looks to me," I said. "Lippy wants you because you owe him money. The cops want you because you might have killed Lola Faithful. Blackstone tolerates you, but if he finds out about Angel he may let some air into your skull."

"Yeah," Victor said. His hands were clenched in front of his chest and he was staring down at his thumbs. "I don't care about myself, Marlowe. But we gotta protect Angel."

"I could tell that," I said. "I could tell just knowing you as I do that your life is a long unbroken sequence of self-sacrifice and concern for others."

"Honest to God, Marlowe. I love that girl. Maybe the only thing I ever loved. Guys would laugh probably, hear me saying something like this, but I'd turn myself in today if it would help her. But I can't because if Blackstone found out about me and Angel he'd have her killed too."

"Well, if you can restrain your passion for self-sacrifice," I said, "and keep your mouth shut and hide out with your Poodle Springs wife until I figure this out . . ."

I let it hang. I didn't have a finish for the sentence myself. Neither did he. We were silent until I dropped him in front of Muriel's place. He took off his hairpiece, put it in my glove compartment and walked wearily up the walk. As he reached the door I saw his shoulders straighten. I put the Olds in gear and drove on toward the house I shared with Linda.

19

"Clayton Blackstone is a very dignified man," Linda said. "I do not believe all that stuff that Muffy's husband told you."

We were having breakfast by the pool in the already solid heat of the desert morning. There was a scent of bougainvillaea on the air and the sound of birds, foraging in the morning before the heat got too bad.

"It's a question of law whether he's her husband," I said. "I think the first marriage precludes those that follow." I sipped my coffee, some sort of Kona roast that Tino had shipped to him. "On the other hand, I'm not up on my bigamy law."

"Clayton Blackstone is a friend of Daddy's," Linda

said. She was wearing a pale blue silk thing that concealed enough of her to be legal, but only that.

"I don't know where Daddy got his money," I said, "but if you have enough of it some of it has to be dirty."

"You think my father has been dishonest?"

"It's not that simple," I said.

"Well, what do you think?"

"I think he probably at least allowed a little dishonesty."

"Oh pooh," Linda said.

Tino came and took away the empty juice glasses.

"Obviously Les, or Larry, or whatever he calls himself, is a compulsive gambler. Obviously he's a fortune hunter. Obviously he's dishonest. Why are you protecting him? Why not simply turn him in to the police?" Linda said. "Report to Mr. Lipshultz where he is, and get to spend some afternoons with me, drinking gimlets, and holding hands, and, um . . . whatever."

"He doesn't understand it, either," I said.

"Les? I should think he wouldn't, the worm, what kind of a man would get himself into this kind of a mess." Linda's eyes were bright with distaste.

"He's addicted," I said.

"To drugs?"

"To risk. He's probably a compulsive gambler, and he has to turn everything into a gamble."

"Why on earth would a man want to do that? Why does someone feel that way about gambling?"

"It's not gambling," I said. "It's risk, the danger of losing, that gets the juices going."

"He likes to lose?" Linda said. The angry glint was gone from her eyes and she was frowning slightly so that the lovely little line appeared horizontally between her perfect eyebrows. She leaned toward me on the chaise, holding her little blue wisp of a garment together at the throat so that she could maintain the semblance of decency and, in the process, keep me from getting out of hand.

"No, but he likes the chance of losing," I said. "It excites him."

"So he gambles and commits bigamy and takes pornographic pictures and maybe murders someone?"

"Things get out of hand," I said. "Now there's too much danger. He's not getting a thrill out of it. Now he's scared. And I don't think he killed the woman in his office."

Linda leaned back against the chaise and chewed on the edge of her lower lip a little, looking at me sideways out of the corners of her eyes.

"You're thinking," I said.

"Umm."

"You're beautiful when you think," I said.

"You understand this man very well," Linda said.

"I'm a detective, lady. I meet a lot of people in trouble."

"Maybe you're a little like this one. Maybe you do the work you do because it's dangerous."

"Like Larry Victor? I get a thrill out of danger?"

"There must be some reason," Linda said, "why you don't stay home and help me spend ten million dollars."

"Maybe I could get a little gold ring grafted onto my neck," I said, "and you could wear me on your charm bracelet."

"You really are impossible, aren't you," Linda said. "Fortunately I find you scrumptious."

"I know that," I said.

20

There was a Santa Ana wind blowing in Hollywood and it had blown the smog out past Catalina. The sky was as blue as a cornflower and the weather was in the low seventies when I parked on Sunset and walked back toward Western to Reno's café. It was just after noon and most of the hookers had broken for lunch. North and east across the Valley past Pasadena I could see the snow on top of the San Gabriel Mountains.

I went into Reno's. It smelled as if they hadn't cleaned the grill in a while. I went to the bar and sat at one end. There were two guys in plaid suits hunched over a notebook at the other end, and in the booth I'd sat in the other day a white-haired guy in a black western-style shirt was feeding drinks to a hard-faced old woman with the faint memory of blonde in her hair. She was wearing bright blue harlequin glasses studded with rhinestones. The old guy's teeth had that perfect even quality that only comes from a store.

There was no one else in the place. The bartender slid down the bar as if he had more time than anyone needed. He was a tall narrow guy with a bald head. Wisps of black hair were carefully plastered over it to make it look worse. His teeth were yellow and he had the color of a man who goes out only at night.

"What'll it be, pal?" he said.

"Rye," I said. "Straight up."

He pulled a bottle from the display rack behind him and poured me a shot of Old Overholt, rang up the cost, put the check on the bar in front of me.

"Lola Faithful come in here much?" I said.

The bartender shrugged and started to move on down the bar. I took a twenty-dollar bill out of my pocket and folded it the long way and let it stand like a small green tent on the bar in front of me. The bartender moved back down the bar toward it.

"Thought you'd want to run a tab," he said.

"I do," I said.

He looked at the twenty and moistened his lips with a tongue the color of a raw oyster.

"Lola Faithful come in here much?" I said.

"Oh, Lola, sure, I didn't get you the first time. Hell, Lola comes in here all the time. Christ, that's what she does. She comes in here."

He grinned with his big yellow teeth, like an old horse. He was looking at the twenty. I picked it up by one end and looked at it poised on my fingertips.

"What can you tell me about her?"

"She drinks Manhattans," he said.

"Anything else?"

"I think she used to be some kind of a hoochie-cooch dancer," he said.

"And?"

"And nothing," he said. "That's all I know."

I nodded.

"Know a guy named Larry Victor?" I said.

"Naw," the bartender said. His eyes followed the movement of the twenty. "Only a few regulars, I know. Most people ain't regulars." He stopped looking at the twenty for a moment and swept the room with a glance.

"Hell," he said, "would you be a regular here?"

"Les Valentine?" I said. He shook his head.

I let the twenty fall from my fingers and slid it over the bar toward him. He picked it up in long fingers and folded it expertly and tucked it into the watch pocket of his tan poplin pants. Then he picked up the bottle of rye and topped off my glass.

"House bonus," he said.

I nodded and he went down the bar and began to polish glasses with a towel better suited to other purposes.

I waited.

The two guys in plaid folded up their notebook and left to make their fortune. The old guy in the booth was succeeding too well with his date. She was drunk already and pawing him. A Mexican kid, maybe ten, came into the bar.

"Shine, Mister?" he said.

"No, thanks," I said.

"Hey, Chico," the bartender said. "How many times I got to tell you, out." He started around the bar.

"Pictures?" the kid said to me.

I shook my head.

"Reefers, maybe? Coke?"

The bartender came around the bar and swiped at the kid with his towel.

"Go on, kid, take a hike."

I took a dollar from my pocket and handed it to the kid.

"Here," I said. "Thanks for asking."

The kid took the bill and dashed for the door.

"You keep coming in here, kid, you're going to end up down to juvie hall, goddammit."

The bartender went back behind the bar shaking his head.

"Beaners," he muttered.

I sipped my rye. The bartender cut up some limes and lemons and stored them in a big-mouthed jar.

The old couple in the booth had another round. She had her head on his shoulder now, her eyes half shut, her mouth dropped open. A fly circled slowly in on the wet spot where my glass had sat. It lazed down close to it, its translucent wings blurred, then it landed and sampled some and rubbed its forefeet together in appreciation. I had another sip of rye.

A red-haired woman came into the bar and glanced around and saw me and came to the bar and sat two stools away. It was the same woman who had played the jukebox during Lola's argument with Victor.

"White wine, Willie," she said.

The bartender got a big jug of wine out of the under-bar refrigerator and poured some in a glass and set it in front of her on a napkin. He put the jug in a sink full of ice, where it was handy, rang up the bill on the register and put it near her on the bar. She picked up the wine and looked at it for a moment and then carefully drank maybe half the glass. She put the glass down on the bar without letting go of the stem and looked at the bartender.

"Ah, Willie," she said. "You can always trust it, can't you?"

"Sure, Val."

She smiled and got out a long thin cigarette with a brown wrapper and looked in her purse, then turned toward me with the cigarette in her mouth, held in place by two fingers.

"Got a light?" she said.

I got a kitchen match out of my coat and managed to snap it into flame with my thumbnail on the first try. I held it steady for her while she leaned forward and put the tip of her cigarette into the flame. She took a deep inhale and let the smoke out slowly as she straightened.

Her hair was red, brighter than any God had ever made, but probably a version of its original shade. She had a soft face in which the lines at the corners of her mouth had deepened over the years into deep parentheses. She wore all the make-up there was and maybe a little no one else knew about. She had on false eyelashes and green eye shadow, and her mouth was made wider than her lips with thick strokes of lipstick. There was a line low on her throat where the make-up stopped short of the collar of her blouse, and the soft flesh under her chin made her neck line blend in with her chin line. Her blouse was white with a frilly collar and her skirt was black and above her knees. Her fingernails were very long and sharp and painted the same harsh red as her lipstick. She wore two large gold hoops dangling from her earlobes. Even in the dim bar I could see fine vertical lines on her upper lip, and the cross-hatching of fine lines around her eyes.

"Wine, cigarettes and a good man," she said. "All anyone can ask of life."

She drank the rest of her wine and gestured with her head for the bartender to pour some more.

"The first two sound all right," I said.

"You don't want a good man?" She laughed, a hoarse, raspy, mannish laugh that ended in a wheeze.

"Not a man's man, I guess," she wheezed as she pushed the laughter back in place. She coughed a little and drank some wine. I smiled encouragingly.

"Wish I could say the same," she said. "Easy to get wine and cigarettes. Hard as hell to find a good man."

She coughed again and drank some wine and picked up the little paper napkin that came with the wine, and patted her lips with it.

"And God knows I've tried a lot of them."

Her wine was gone. She glanced at the bartender, but he was looking at the old couple in the booth.

"Willie," I said, "lady needs a refill. Put it on my tab."

Willie decanted the jug wine without comment. Rang it up on my bill.

"Thanks," she said. "You seem too nice a guy to be hanging out here."

"I was going to say that about you," I said.

"Sure you were," she said. "Then you were going to put me in pictures, weren't you."

"If I'd been in the picture business a few years back," I said. I could see my face in the bar. It had the innocent oily look of a coyote stealing a chicken.

"You look like a guy could get things done if he wanted."

"I was here the other day, and saw you," I said. "There was an argument. Man and woman were hollering at each other and you were playing the jukebox."

Val drank some of her wine. Her cigarette had burned away to an unsmokable roach in the ashtray. She dug another from her purse and I had the kitchen match ready. Marlowe the courtier. I'd have made a great manservant.

"Yeah," she said, "Lola and Larry. Are they a trip? What I mean about men, you know."

"What were they fighting about?" I said. She got

some wine in. She was drinking it as if the Four Horsemen of the Apocalypse had been sighted in Encino.

Val's shrug was elaborate. Everything about her was exaggerated, like a female impersonator.

"What's your name, honey?"

"Marlowe," I said.

"You ever been in love, Marlowe?"

"As we speak," I said.

"Well, wait'll it goes sour," she said. I nodded at Willie and he filled her wine glass.

"When it goes sour, it's like rotting roses. It reeks."

"Lola and Larry?" I said.

"For a while, a while back." She shook her head in a slow, showy sweep. "But he dumped her."

"What was the fight the other day specifically about?" I said.

"She had something she knew," Val said. "She was going to get even, I guess."

She drank.

"A woman spurned," she said heavily. "We were made for love. We can get pretty poisonous when it turns."

She drank again. A little of the wine dribbled from the corner of her mouth. She dabbed at it again with the paper place napkin.

"She had something on him," I said.

"Sure," Val said. "And she was going to make him pay."

"What'd she have?" I said.

"Hell, Marlowe, I don't know. There's always something. Probably something on you if somebody looks hard." She laughed her wheezy laugh again, gestured at me with her wine glass.

"Prosit," she said and laughed some more. The rim of the wine glass was smeared with her lipstick.

"You know Larry too," I said.

She nodded and fished in her purse, taking things out. Compact, lipstick, a crumpled tissue, chewing gum, rosary beads, a nail file.

"You got any quarters, Marlowe?"

I slid a five at Willie.

"Quarters," I said.

He made change and put the quarters in five neat piles of four on the bar in front of me.

"You're a gennleman," Val said and took a pile and walked to the jukebox. In a minute she came back and sat on her bar stool as the first wail of a country song came on about a woman who loved a man and he done her wrong. Mood music.

"What was you asking me?" Val said.

"Did you know Larry very well?" I said, carefully. Drunks are fragile creatures. They need to be carried like a very full glass, tip either way and they spill all over. I knew about drunks. I'd spent half my life talking to drunks in bars like this one. Who'd you see, what'd you hear? Have another drink. Sure, on me, Marlowe, the big spender, the lush's pal, drink up, lush. You're lonely and I'm your pal.

"Sure, I know Larry. Everybody knows Larry. The man with the camera. The man with the pictures."

She finished her wine. Willie poured some more. He was not a boy to miss the main chance, old Willie. She needed another cigarette. I took one out of her pack on the bar and lit it and handed it to her. Maybe I wouldn't have made a good manservant. Maybe I would have made a good gigolo. Maybe I didn't want to think about that. Maybe that hit too close to home.

"I used to pose for Larry, you know."

"I can believe that," I said.

Val nodded and stared at me. "Wasn't that long ago I still looked good with my clothes off."

"I can believe that too," I said.

"Well, I did."

"Larry usually take women's pictures with their clothes off?"

"Sure," Val said. "Larry looked at more nudes than my gynecologist."

She was pleased as hell to have said that and laughed

and wheezed until she got coughing and I had to beat her on the back to get her to stop.

"Wise old Dr. Larry," she gasped. "Used to peddle the stuff around the boulevard when it was harder to get. Now he wholesales it, I guess. I don't know. Who cares about dirty pictures anymore. You know?"

"Get 'em on any newsstand," I said. "Did he do any legit photography? Fashion stuff?"

Val repressed a belch, touched her fingertips to her lips automatically.

" 'Scuse me," she said brightly. The jukebox moaned out another sad country ballad. The old couple in the booth got up and stumbled out, arms around each other's waist, her left hand in his back pocket, her head on his shoulder. Val was still smiling at me.

"Did he ever do fashion stuff?" I said.

"Who?"

"Larry."

"Oh, yeah, fashion stuff." She paused a long time. I waited. Time is different for drunks.

"Nooo," Val said. "He never did none. He said he did, but I never saw any or knew about anybody he photographed."

She had trouble with *photographed*.

"Where'd Lola live?" I said.

"Lola?"

"Yeah."

"What about her?"

"Where'd she live?"

"Kenmore," Val said. "222 Kenmore, just below Franklin."

"She in any trouble lately?"

"Naw, Lola, she was fine. Had some alimony checks coming in every month. Me, I got to go to court to get mine. I'm in court more than the judge, for chrissake."

"Nobody mad at her or anything?"

Val grinned. Her lipstick had gotten blurred from frequent trips to the rim of her glass.

"Jes' Larry," Lola said.

"Because of the fight they had."

"Un huh."

Val drank some more wine. Some of it dribbled down her chin. She paid it no mind. She was singing along now softly to the mournful music.

"You wanna dance?" she said. "Used to dance like a swan."

"They're good dancers," I said.

"You don't have to," she said, "if you don't want." She was swaying a little to the music.

"As long as it's slow," I said. I stood and put out my arms. She slid off the stool and wavered a bit, got centered and stepped in close to me. She was wearing enough perfume to stop a charging rhino, and it hadn't come in a little crystal flagon. She put her left hand in mine, and her right lightly behind my left shoulder, and we began to move in the empty barroom to the lonesome country sound.

"Ain't supposed to be dancing in here," Willie said from behind the bar. But he said it weakly and neither of us paid him any attention. It was dim in the bar and most of the light reflected off the bar mirror and the bright array of bottles in front of it. We danced among the tables and along the booths, down toward the front where a little sunlight filtered through the dirty windows. In addition to the old cooking smell there was the fresh, delusive smell of booze that made the air seem cooler. Val put her head against my shoulder as we danced in a slow circle around the room, and she sang the song that we danced to. She knew the lyrics. She probably knew all the lyrics to all the sad songs, just like she knew just how many four-ounce glasses of white wine you got out of a half-gallon jug. The music stopped. The quarters she'd put in were used up, but still we danced, with her head on my shoulder. She sang a little more of the song and then she was quiet and all the sound was the shuffle of our feet in the empty room. Val started to cry, softly, without moving her head from my shoulder. I didn't say anything. Outside on Sunset somebody was power-shifting a car with dual exhausts and the snarling pitch changes bored through our silence. I danced Val gently past a table and four chairs and as I did she suddenly went limp on me.

I spread my feet and bent my knees and slid both my arms around her under hers and edged her to a booth. She was as limp as an overcooked noodle, her legs splayed and dragging. I bowed my back and heaved her into the booth and arranged her with as much dignity as she had left. Behind the bar Willie watched without comment.

"No need to help," I said. "She can't weigh more than a two-door Buick. I'll be fine."

"Drunks are heavy," Willie said.

I got out another twenty; they were getting scarce in my wallet. I walked over to the bar and gave it to Willie.

"When she comes around," I said, "put her in a cab."

"When she comes around," Willie said, "she's going to want to drink another gallon of white wine, until she passes out again."

"Okay," I said. "Then let her do that when she comes to."

"You spending an awful lot of dough on an old wino floozie," Willie said.

"I got a rich wife," I said.

I paid the bar bill with my last twenty and went out of there into the hot, hard, unkind sun.

21

Number 222 was on the left side as you drive up Kenmore toward Franklin. It sat up on a small lawn, its front door barely visible under the overhang of the porch roof. It was one of those comfortable cool bungalows with big front porches that they used to build at about the time that L.A. was a sprawling comfortable place with a lot of sunshine and no smog. People used to sit on those porches in the evening and sip iced tea and watch the neighbors water their lawns with long loping sweeps of a hose. They used to sleep with the front door open and the screen door held with a simple hook. They used to listen to the radio, and sometimes on Sundays they'd take one of the interurban trains out to the beach for a picnic. I parked around the corner on Franklin and walked back.

The lawn had gone to hell in front of the place. The grass was so high it had gone to seed. The house needed paint and the screen had pulled loose in the front screen door in several places and the screening had curled up like the collar points on an old shirt. The front door was locked, but the frame had shrunk up so that it didn't take much to get in. I put my shoulder against the frame and the flat of my hand against the door and pushed in both directions at once and I was in.

The place smelled like places do that have been closed up empty for a while. To the right through an archway was the sitting room. There was a couch there, half sprung, with a crocheted throw on it, turned back as if someone had been under it and just gotten up. Opposite was a big old television set on legs. On top was a square apothecary jar full of small colorful hard candies, individually wrapped in cellophane. The thin blue Navaho rug on the floor was worn threadbare, and a coffee table made of bent bamboo was shoved over near the head of the couch. There were some movie magazines and a true romance magazine and an ashtray full of filter-tipped cigarette butts. The late afternoon light as it sifted through the dusty muslin curtains picked up dust motes in the air.

The cops would have seen all this. They'd have looked at everything like they do, and anything that mattered would be down in a box in property storage with a case tag on it. Still, they didn't know all the things I knew, and I was hoping I might see something that wouldn't have meant anything to them. It wasn't in the sitting room. I moved to the kitchen. It had gotten dark. I snapped on a light. If the cops had a watch on the place they'd have seen me come in and would be here by now. The neighbors would just think I was another cop.

There was a half loaf of bread and an unwrapped stick of butter sitting on a saucer in the refrigerator. In the freezer was a bottle of vodka. There were three or four limes turning yellow in a Pyrex dish on the kitchen counter, and some instant coffee in a jar in the cupboard. There was a shrunken bar of hand soap on the rim of the sink. That was it. No flour, no salt, no meat, no potatoes. Just bread and butter and vodka and instant coffee. The limes were probably for scurvy. I looked behind the refrigerator and under the sink and inside the empty cabinets. I took the strainer out of the sink and looked down into the drain as best I could. I checked the oven, examined the linoleum around the edges to see if anything had been slipped down underneath. I unrolled the window shades and pulled over a chair and climbed up and looked inside the glass globe on the kitchen light.

While I was doing that a voice behind me said, "Hold that pose, Sailor."

I had a gun in a shoulder rig but it might as well have been in the trunk of my car for all the good it did me standing on a chair with my hands over my head. I stood still.

"Now put your hands on top of your head and step down off of there," the voice said. It was a soft voice with no accent but a faint foreign lilt in it.

I managed to keep my hands on my head and get off the chair without dislocating a kneecap.

"Turn around," the voice said. There was nothing gentle in the softness; it was the softness of a snake's hiss. I turned around.

There were two of them. One was a California Beach Boy, lots of tan, lots of muscle, just enough brains to know the handle end of a blackjack. He had on white pants and a flowered shirt and he was holding a Colt .45 automatic like the army used to issue. He held it Southern California casual, half turned over on his palm, not aimed at anything special, but generally toward me. The other guy was shorter and slimmer. He wore a black suit, black shirt and narrow black tie and his movements were very graceful. Merely standing still he looked like a dancer. He had a thick black moustache and longish black hair brushed straight back. His dark eyes had no feeling in them at all. The voice belonged to him.

"So, Sailor, why don't you sort of tell me about who you are and how come you're standing on a chair in the kitchen here. Stuff like that."

"Who's asking?" I said.

He smiled without any feeling at all and pointed at the beach boy's automatic.

"Oh," I said, "him. I've met him before. He doesn't impress me."

"Tough," he said. He looked at the beach boy. "Everybody's tough," he said. He'd have been more impressed if I wiggled my ears.

"You want me to shoot some corner of him, Eddie? So he'll know we mean it?"

Eddie shook his head.

"My name's Garcia," he said, "Eddie Garcia." He nodded at the beach boy. "This is J.D. Pretty, isn't he?"

"Beautiful," I said. "If he pulls the trigger on that thing can he hit what it's pointed at?"

"From this close?" Eddie smiled. The effect was of light passing over a flat stone surface for a moment. The surface never changed.

"We represent a very important person who has an

interest in this house and its occupant and we wish to report to him what you were doing in here, and why. We would rather do that than deliver your body to him in the trunk of our car."

I nodded. "Who's your man?" I said.

Garcia shook his head. J.D. thumbed the hammer back on the Colt. I looked at Garcia. J.D. didn't matter. Garcia's empty obsidian eyes gazed blankly back at me. I knew he'd do it.

"My name's Marlowe," I said. "I'm a private eye working on a case. How about you take me to your VIP and I tell him the rest. Maybe our interests would mesh."

"You know who owns this house?" Garcia said.

"Woman named Lola," I said. "She's dead."

Garcia nodded. He looked at me. There was no expression. I assumed he was thinking.

"Okay," he said. "You got a piece under your left arm. I'll have to take it. And I want to see some ID."

"Wallet's in my left hip pocket," I said.

Garcia drifted in, took the gun out of my shoulder holster, lifted the wallet off the hip and drifted out, all it seemed in one seamless motion. He dropped the gun in his side pocket and flipped open my wallet. He looked at the photostat of my license for a moment and then shut my wallet and handed it back to me. I took my hands off my head and took the wallet and slipped it in my hip pocket.

"Okay, Sailor," he said. "You ride with us."

We went out in single file: Garcia, me, and J.D. Garcia got in behind the wheel of a Lincoln. J.D. and I got in the back. We rolled west on Franklin with the windows up and the air conditioning on. No one spoke. At Laurel Canyon we went down to Sunset and continued on Sunset as the houses got bigger and the lawns more empty through West Hollywood and Beverly Hills to Bel Air. We went in past the Bel Air gate and the private police booth and wound along into Bel Air until Garcia stopped the Lincoln in front of a pair of ten-foot spiked iron gates with gilded points. He rolled down the window as a guy in a blue blazer and grey slacks stepped out of the sentry box next to the gate. The guy looked in, saw Garcia and went back in the sentry box. I could see him pick up a phone, and in a moment the gates opened slowly and Garcia drove us through. There was no house in sight yet. Just a winding driveway paved in some sort of white material that might have been crushed oyster shells. The headlights played over a forest of flowering shrubs and short trees that I couldn't identify in the dark. We went down a small hill, wound up a somewhat higher one and turned a corner. The house that rose up in front of us wasn't anywhere near big enough to hold all of California. Probably not more than the entire population of Los Angeles comfortably. It was lit from the outside with spotlights: white masonry with gables and towers and narrow Tudor windows with diamond panes. There was a vast porte-cochère in front, and when we pulled in under it and stopped, two more guys in blazers appeared to open the doors.

"You work for Walt Disney?" I said.

"It's a little showy," Garcia said. He got out of the car. So did I. J.D. got out after me.

"Wait here, J.D.," Garcia said.

"How long you gonna be, Eddie?" J.D. said. "I got stuff I'm supposed to do tonight."

Garcia paused and turned his head slowly and looked at J.D. He didn't say anything. J.D. shifted from one foot to the other. Then he tried a smile.

"No rush, Eddie," he said. "Anything else I got going tonight can wait."

Garcia nodded and walked toward the front door. He seemed to expend no effort walking; he seemed to glide. I went after him. One of The Blazers opened the right-hand half of the double front door. It was ten feet high and studded with wrought-iron nail heads.

Inside was a stone floor the length of the house with French doors in the distance that led to something leafy. There was a vast curving staircase rising on the left side of the central corridor and doors opened to the right and left. The ceiling rose thirty or forty feet, and from it hung an enormous iron chandelier in which candles flickered. Real candles, on a giant iron wheel. There were probably a hundred of them. They provided the only light in the hall. On the stone floor there was an Oriental runner that reached the length of the floor and on the wall were tapestries of medieval knights on plump horses with delicate legs.

The front door closed behind us. A butler appeared. He opened one of the doors on the right-hand wall and held it open.

"Follow me, please," he said.

We went through a library with bookshelves filled to the 15-foot ceilings and giant candles burning in 8-foot candlesticks. There was a fireplace that I could have ridden a horse into. To the right of the fireplace another door opened and we followed the butler through into some sort of space that, had it been three times smaller, might have been somebody's office. The far wall was all glass and opened out onto a pool and beyond, the spotlit gardens. The pool had been built to look like some sort of jungle pool with vines and plants dripping practically into it and a rock-strewn waterfall at the far end splashing down into the lapis lazuli water. There

was a bar along another wall, a television set, an illumi-
nated globe almost as big as the original, green leather
furniture of the thick-sofa, club-chair variety scattered
over a green marble floor, with here and there Oriental
throw rugs to stand on if your feet got tired. On the
right wall, behind a desk big enough to land helicop-
ters on, wearing an actual red velvet smoking jacket
with black silk lapels, was a hatchet-faced man with
ice-white hair cut very short, and that phony-looking
tan that everybody in Southern California thinks you
have to have to prove that you don't live where there's
smog. I had seen his picture on a wall once.

Hatchet Face was smoking a white clay pipe with a
stem about a foot long, the kind you see in old Dutch
paintings. He looked at me the way a wolf looks at a
lamb chop and put the stem in his mouth and puffed.

"If you meet people bowling ten pins in the mountains," I said, "don't drink anything they offer."

Hatchet Face didn't change expression. Maybe he
couldn't.

Garcia said, "Guy's name is Marlowe, Mr. Blackstone. He thinks he's tough, and he thinks he's funny."

Blackstone's voice sounded like someone pouring
sand out of a funnel.

"I don't think he's either," he said. There was nothing there for me; I let it pass.

163

"We found him in that house on Kenmore," Garcia said. "He was tossing it."

Blackstone nodded. He still had the long stem in his mouth, the bowl cradled in his right hand.

"Why?" he said.

"Says he's a PI. Got a California license, had a gun."

"What else?"

"Didn't want to say. Said he wanted to talk with you. I figured you might want to talk with him."

Blackstone nodded, once. It was an approval nod. Garcia didn't look like he cared whether Blackstone approved. On the other hand, Blackstone didn't look like he cared if Garcia cared. These weren't people who wore their hearts on their sleeves. Blackstone shifted his stare to me. His eyes were very pale blue, almost grey.

"What else?" he said in his sandy whisper.

"I was told a woman named Lola lived there," I said. "She popped up in a case I was working on."

"And?"

"And I thought I'd look over her house, see what it told me."

Blackstone waited. I waited. Eddie Garcia waited. You had the sense from Eddie that he could wait forever.

"And?"

"And what's your interest?" I said.

Blackstone looked from me to Garcia and back.

"Perhaps I should have Eddie teach you some manners," he said.

"Perhaps you should stop trying to scare me to death and share a little information. Maybe we're not adversaries."

"Adversaries." Blackstone made a sound which he probably thought was a laugh. "An intellectual peeper."

"My wife reads aloud to me sometimes," I said.

Blackstone made his sound again. "With a wife that can read," he said. "You know that Lola Faithful is dead?"

"Yeah, shot in the head with a small-caliber gun at close range, in a photographer's office on Western Ave."

"So what's that got to do with you?" Blackstone said.

"I found the body."

Blackstone leaned back a little in his chair. He pushed his lower lip out maybe half a millimeter.

"You," he said.

"Yeah, and that made me sort of wonder about who shot her."

"Have you a theory?"

"Nothing as strong as a theory," I said.

Blackstone stared at me for a moment, then he looked at Garcia, then back at me.

"I too would like to know who murdered her," he said.

"I had a sense you might be interested," I said. "About the time your boys threw down on me in Lola's house. And I figure you don't know much about it or why would you have a couple of guys staking the place out. And I figure it's important as hell to you or why would one of the guys be your top boy."

"What else do you figure?" Blackstone whispered.

"It's what I don't figure that matters. I don't figure whether you're interested in who killed Lola because of Lola, or because of who killed her."

Again Blackstone looked at me with his expressionless gaze. Again he glanced at Garcia, which was probably as close as he got to indecision.

"I don't know Lola Faithful," he said.

"So it's who killed her that you're worried about," I said.

"Cops like the photographer," he said.

"Cops like the obvious," I said. "Usually they're right."

"You like him?" Blackstone said.

"No."

"Why not?"

"He doesn't seem the type."

"That's all?" Blackstone said.

"Yep."

"You ever a cop?"

"Yeah," I said. "Now I'm not. Cops can't decide that someone doesn't seem the type. They've seen too many axe murderers that look like choirboys. They don't have time to think if someone's the type. They have to throw everything in the hopper and take what sifts through."

"You seem a romantic, Mr. Marlowe."

"And you don't, Mr. Blackstone."

"Not often," Blackstone said.

"Did you know, I know your daughter?" I said.

Blackstone didn't say anything. It was what he did instead of showing surprise.

"I didn't know that," he said.

"She's married to the photographer," I said.

There was no sound in the room, except the nearly inaudible sigh of breath that Blackstone let out through his nose. It was only one sigh. Then silence. It was a risk telling him. He might not know the connection between Les and Larry. He might actually be the tooth fairy, too. Sooner or later he'd find out that I knew Muriel, and that I knew both Les and Larry, and if it was dangerous to tell him now it would be more dangerous later when he knew I was holding out on him. I could feel Garcia behind me, with my gun in his pocket. Blackstone laid down the long silly pipe and put both his steepled hands under his chin and looked at me silently.

"Mr. Marlowe," he said, "maybe you and I should have a drink."

22

I was sitting in one of the green leather chairs.

"Les owed a guy money," I said. I had a big Scotch and soda with Scotch from a curved crystal decanter and soda from a siphon. Blackstone had the same. Garcia had nothing; he lounged against the wall near the bar as if time had stopped and would start only when he said so. He didn't listen or not listen. He simply existed over there by the bar in total relaxation.

"And the guy hired me to locate Les for him."

"Who's the guy?" Blackstone said.

I shook my head. "Client's got a right to be anonymous," I said.

"Where the hell do you think you are, Marlowe?" Blackstone said. "In court someplace?"

"Guy in my business hasn't got much to sell: a little muscle, a little guts, some privacy." I crossed one leg over the other and rested my drink on the top knee. "If I'm going to be in this business I can't go around spilling my guts to every loonigan I meet."

"I'm hardly a loonigan, Marlowe."

"Sure," I said, "you're a citizen and a half. Pillar of the community, or what there is of it out here. Bet you're on the board at a lot of important places."

Blackstone nodded.

"Which is why," I said, "you have Eddie Garcia walking behind you everywhere you go."

"A man makes enemies, Marlowe."

"And Eddie takes care of them," I said.

"Whenever necessary," he said.

"Sure," I said.

Across the room Garcia never moved. We could have been discussing the price of aldermen for all the difference it seemed to make to him.

"Anyway." I sipped a little Scotch; it seemed to seep into my mouth and spread gently. You could probably spend my weekly earnings for a bottle of this stuff. "It seemed simple enough."

"Only it wasn't," Blackstone said.

"No," I said. "I started with his wife, your daughter. She said he was on location doing stills for a movie production. While I was there I noticed a fashion photo of a model I recognized with Les's name on it."

"You checked the movie company," Blackstone said. "They never heard of him. You checked the model. She never heard of him."

"Eddie's been busy," I said.

Blackstone mercly nibbled at his drink.

"So I went back and searched his house."

Blackstone said, "My daughter's house."

"Probably your house," I said. "I'll bet old Les didn't buy it."

"I gave it to her," Blackstone said.

I nodded. "In his drawer I found a parking ticket. I ran that back, found the address and found a photographer named Larry Victor in the building at the address. I braced him. He said he knew Les but that Les was out of town. I followed him to a bar, watched him have a fight with Lola Faithful. I lost Larry, went back to search his office."

Blackstone interrupted. "Why?"

"Why not?" I said. "I didn't have anything else. He said he knew Valentine."

Blackstone nodded.

"I walked in and there was Lola with her brains on the floor."

"And this guy Larry?" Blackstone said.

"Is Valentine," I said, "with a wig and contact lenses."

"Where is he?"

"I don't know," I said.

"Well," Blackstone said, "you have accomplished much, but not enough. Do you know why Valentine masquerades as Victor?"

"Or vice versa," I said. "No, I don't."

Blackstone nodded.

"Two things I'd like to know," I said.

I drank some more of the Scotch and paused to admire it.

"One, why were you looking for Valentine, and two, why did you have Garcia watching Lola's house?"

"You seem to have been candid with me, Marlowe, up to a point. I'm looking for Valentine because he's been away and my daughter was worried. As for Lola Faithful, a woman of that name attempted to blackmail my daughter."

"About what?"

Blackstone shook his head.

"My daughter did not say, and I did not ask. I told

my daughter that I would have Eddie speak to her. Eddie was away on business for a day or so, and when he returned he went to call on Lola only to find that she had been murdered."

Blackstone sampled his Scotch. It didn't seem to amaze him. He was used to it.

"You can understand my interest," he said.

I nodded.

"And your daughter?"

"I merely told her that the woman had died. I did not ask her anything."

We were quiet then, inhaling the Scotch, speculating about each other's intentions.

Finally I said, "How do you feel about Les Valentine, Mr. Blackstone?"

Blackstone held the glass of Scotch between his palms and looked into it and turned it slowly as if he wanted to admire it from all its angles. He took some air in slowly through his nose and let it out more slowly.

"He's a liar, a womanizer, a petty thief, an opportunist, a fool, an unsuccessful, probably compulsive, gambler, with no more spine than a dandelion. And my daughter loves him. As long as she does he is one of nature's noblemen to me. I will support him. I will intercede with those who bear him ill will. As long as he is married to my daughter, he is family."

"Even though he's a wrong Gee," I said.

"I am not much of a father, Mr. Marlowe. I have only my daughter. Her mother is long since gone. I indulge my daughter entirely, doubtless for selfish reasons. If she wishes to be married to a wrong Gee then he will become, so to speak, my wrong Gee."

"The wrong Gee is home," I said. "I delivered him myself."

"So you weren't telling me everything," Blackstone said.

"I never said I was."

"You're an interesting man, Marlowe. You wouldn't tell me that until you decided what I'd do with the information."

I didn't say anything.

"I can admire that, Marlowe. But do not make the mistake of confusing admiration with patience. I can eliminate you by nodding my head. And if it suits my purposes I will."

"Anybody can eliminate anybody, Mr. Blackstone. Once you realize that, it all gets into perspective."

"Where did you find him?"

"He was in his office," I lied. "I told him the cops would be after him any minute and he came with me."

"Where had he been?"

I shrugged. "He didn't say."

Blackstone put the glass to his lips, discovered it was empty, gestured, without looking, to Garcia. Eddie was there with the decanter and siphon. He looked at me. I shook my head. Eddie was back at the bar.

"Be careful, Marlowe. I'm not a playful man. So be very careful."

"Sure," I said. "You don't mind if I nibble on a turnip once in a while."

"Take him home, Eddie," Blackstone said. "When you get there give him back his gun."

"Lola's place would be fine," I said. "I didn't finish searching it."

Blackstone almost smiled.

"Take him where he wants to go, Eddie."

This time J.D. drove and Eddie rode in back with me. When we got to Kenmore Eddie reached in his side pocket and got my gun. J.D. stopped in front of Lola's house. It was silent. The street was dark. There was a high pale moon shining straight down on us. Garcia handed me my gun.

"You're a piece of work, Marlowe," he said. "I'll give you that."

I stowed the gun under my arm and got out of the car.

J.D. slid it into gear. I gave it the gunman's salute as they drove away.

23

It was 3:37 on my wristwatch, by moonlight, when I came out of Lola Faithful's house. I hadn't found anything, but on the other hand no one else had come and pointed a gun at me. It was too late to go home. I drove slowly. Hollywood was empty, the houses blank and aimless, all the colors altered by the moon glow. Only the neon lights along Sunset were still awake. They were always awake. Bright, hearty and fake, full of Hollywood promises. The days come and go. The neon endures.

I tried to figure out why I was here, alone, in the night on Sunset musing about neon. I had a client, but he sure as hell hadn't hired me to protect Valentine and look for whoever killed Lola. I hadn't slept in a while. I hadn't eaten in a while, and the rye for lunch and the Scotch for supper had worn off, leaving me feeling like something that belonged on Sunset Boulevard at 3:30 in the morning with no place to go. I had a beautiful wife at home in a comfortable bed, sleeping with one arm across her forehead and her mouth open only a fraction. If I got into bed with her now she would roll toward me and put one arm around me. What the hell difference did it make if she owned the bed? What the hell difference did it make if Les Valentine had killed Lola Faithful? Why not let the cops sort it out? At Western Ave I turned up toward Hollywood Boulevard. I didn't have any purpose. I wasn't going anywhere. What the hell difference did it make where I drove? I drove past Larry's building. Ten yards past it I slowed, and U-turned, and cruised back. Something had moved in the doorway of Larry's building. Probably just a bum staying out of the moonlight. Why not take a second look? It didn't matter.

I stopped in front of the building and got a flashlight out of the glove compartment and shined it in the doorway. Huddled back, trying to avoid the light, was Angel, the other wife. I switched off the flash and got out of the car, and when I did she dashed out of the doorway and headed up Western toward Hollywood. What

I needed, a foot race. I took a deep inhale and headed out after her. I caught her after she had rounded the corner at Hollywood and was heading west. I might not have caught her at all but she broke one of the high heels on her shoes.

"It's me," I said, "Marlowe, the guy that drove off with Larry."

She was breathing very hard, and crying a little from fear, and didn't quite get who I was. I held her arms while she tried to pull away.

"Marlowe," I said, "your pal, your protector, your confidant. I won't hurt you."

She struggled less, then even less, and finally stood, her breath going in and out hard, her shoulders shaking, the tears running down her face. I still held her wrists, but she had stopped trying to hit me, and she wasn't trying to pull away.

"It's me," I said again, "Marlowe the moonlight knight. The shabby savior of ladies in doorways."

I was so tired I was dopey.

"Where's Larry?" she said.

I didn't answer. Instead I looked at the spotlight that was suddenly in my eyes from the car that had swung around the corner from Western and pulled up over the curb beside us.

"Hold it right there," a voice said. It was a cop voice,

a little bored, a little tough. They came out of the spot-light on either side of me.

"Hands on the car, Jack," one of them said.

I put my hands on the roof of the car. One of them kicked my legs apart and patted me down. He took the gun from under my arm. Made me wonder why I carried it, people kept taking it away. Then the cop stepped back away from me.

"Got some ID?" he said.

I fished my wallet out again and handed it over and the cop looked at the contents in the light of the spotlight. They were both plainclothes, one fat with his tie snugged up around his neck but off center. The other one, the one doing the talking, was a tall, loose-built guy with glasses. He had on jeans and a tee shirt and wore his gun inside the belt of his jeans in front.

"My name's Bob Kane," he said as he handed me back my wallet. "You mind telling me why you were chasing this lady?"

"I wanted to give her a ride home," I said.

Kane smiled happily.

"Hear that, Gordy?" he said to his fat partner. "Guy just wanted to drive her home."

Gordy had his gun still out but was holding it at his side pointed at the ground.

"No shit," Gordy said. He was wearing a wide-brimmed panama hat with a big flowered band.

"She didn't seem to want to ride home," Kane said. "She kind of looked to be running like hell to get away from you."

"She didn't recognize me," I said.

"You know this guy?" Kane said. His glasses had big round lenses and his eyes were pleasant and heartless behind them, enlarged a little.

Angel nodded. "I know him," she said.

"So how come you were running?" Kane said.

"Like he says, I didn't recognize him."

"How you know him?" Kane said.

"He's a . . . a friend of my husband's."

"Really," Kane said. "That so, Marlowe?"

"I know him," I said.

"Yeah?" Kane stepped back and leaned against the door of the unmarked police car. He folded his long arms and looked at us for a while.

"Marlowe," he said. "Aren't you the guy found the body in her husband's office?"

"Yeah," I said. This wasn't going well, and I had a sense it wasn't going to get better.

"And now you're down hanging around his office and you just happen to run into his wife and chase her and she runs because she doesn't recognize you."

"Exactly," I said.

"If I was a smart copper," Kane said, "I wouldn't be out here around four o'clock in the morning on stakeout. So this is probably too deep for me, but it looks kind of a funny set of circumstances, if you follow me."

"You're too modest," I said.

"Yeah, probably am, been a failing of mine," Kane said. "You aren't planning to go anywhere far, are you, Marlowe?"

I shrugged.

"You want this guy to give you a ride home, Mrs. Victor?"

Angel nodded.

"Fine," Kane said. "Go ahead."

"Bob," Gordy said, "you oughta haul them in."

"For what?" Kane said.

"Hell, for questioning, hold them until morning, let the lieutenant talk with them."

"Lady's worried about her husband," Kane said. "We'll let him take her home."

"Damn it, Bob," Gordy said.

"Gordy," Kane said, "one of us is a sergeant and one of us isn't. You remember whether it's me or you?"

"You, Bob."

Kane nodded.

"Okay, why don't you go ahead and drive Mrs. Victor on home, Mr. Marlowe. We'll be moseying along behind just to sort of keep track."

He handed me back my gun, I put it under my arm so it would be there when the next guy wanted to take it away, and Angel and I went on down to my car and pulled away. In the rearview mirror I saw the headlights of the unmarked car fall in behind us.

24

"Where's Larry?" Angel said. She was small on the front seat beside me. The dashboard clock said 4:07.

"He's safe," I said.

"I can't wait to see him," she said.

"Can't," I said. "You'd lead the cops right to him."

"Where is he?" she said.

"It's better not to tell you," I said.

"I'm his wife, Mr. Marlowe." She turned in the seat toward me.

"That's why the cops are following you," I said.

"Following?"

"You think they just happened by?" I said. "They have a tail on you."

She turned in the seat and stared back at the head-lights behind us.

"Following me?"

It was as if the last half hour hadn't happened.

"Yes, Ma'am," I said.

"Is he all right?" she said. She turned back from staring at the tail and tucked a leg up under herself and leaned an arm against the back of the seat. As she spoke she bent toward me a little.

"He's fine, Angel. He's safe. He misses you."

She nodded. "I miss him."

We were the only cars on the road as we drove toward Venice. The cops lounged along three or four car lengths behind us.

"Who are you?" Angel said.

"Marlowe," I said. "I'm a private detective on a case."

"Are you a friend of Larry's?"

"I just met him once before, the night we ran out on the cops."

"So why are you helping him?"

"Beats me," I said.

"That's no answer," she said. The cop headlights behind us lit most of the interior of my car. In the light her eyes were wide and dark and full of sweetness.

"You're right," I said. "I don't think he killed the

woman, but he seems to me the kind of guy that might have a little trouble in his background. Not a tough guy, and not connected. The kind of guy the cops will nail. They'll try him at a night session in Bay City and have him sitting in Chino looking at twenty years to life without ever figuring out how he got there."

"Larry wouldn't kill anyone."

"No," I said. "I don't think so either. Are you married to him?"

Angel nodded. There was pride in that nod, and contentment, and something more, something protective, the way a young mother nods when you ask if that's her baby.

"Almost four years," she said.

"Ever hear of a guy named Les Valentine?" I said.

"No."

"Woman named Muriel Blackstone?"

"No."

We were on Wilshire and when it ran out against the Pacific we turned left and drove along the empty beachfront. The moonlight on the waves emphasized how empty the ocean was, and endless, rolling in from Zanzibar.

"Larry's in trouble, isn't he?"

"He's wanted for murder," I said.

"But he didn't do that. He's in some other kind

of trouble," she said. "The kind that brought you to him."

In the moonlight the buildings looked stately, like Moorish castles, the peeling paint and crumbled stucco smoothed out.

"He is, isn't he, Mr. Marlowe?"

"There's a gambler named Lipshultz," I said. "Larry owes him money. He hired me to find him."

She nodded, a nod of confirmation.

"He's had trouble before, hasn't he?" I said.

"He's an artist, Mr. Marlowe. He's imaginative. Many people have said he's a genius with a camera."

"And?" I said.

"And he's impulsive, he's not good with rules. He feels something, he does it. He has an artistic temperament."

"So he bets hunches," I said.

"Yes."

"And they sometimes don't pay off."

"No, they don't. But he has to be free to follow his intuition, don't you see. To limit him is to stifle him."

"He ever been in other kinds of trouble?"

She was silent for a bit, looking out at the silver ocean rolling slowly toward us. On the beach below, above the tide line, some bums were sleeping, clutching their scraps of belongings.

"I think he's had some trouble with women."

"Like what?" I said.

"I don't know, he never said. I don't question him."

"Why not?" I said.

"I love him," she said. As if it answered all the questions.

"So what makes you think there was trouble with women?"

"There were phone calls for him from a woman, and when he hung up he was angry."

"Un huh."

"And . . ." She looked at her lap for a moment, where she had folded her hands. I waited, listening to the wheels murmur over the asphalt.

"And?" I said.

"And there was a picture, I saw."

I waited.

"It was a picture of a woman. She was undressed and posing . . ." She stared harder at her hands. If the light had been better I think I'd have seen her blushing.

"Suggestively?" I said.

"Yes." She said it so softly I could barely hear.

"And you didn't ask him about it?" I said.

"No. It was from the time in Larry's life before he met me. He had a right to that time. It had nothing to do with me."

"You trust him?"

"In the way you mean, yes. He loves me, too."

"He sure as hell ought to," I said.

We pulled up behind the house where she and Larry lived . . . when Larry wasn't living with his other wife in Poodle Springs. She got out her side and I got out mine and came around. The cops stopped a little ways behind us.

"I'll walk you to the door," I said.

"No need," she said. There was the lilt of anxiety in her voice.

"Just to see that you get in safe," I said. "I'm in love too, with my wife."

Angel smiled suddenly, like sunrise after a rainy night.

"That's lovely," she said. "Isn't it."

"Yes," I said.

We walked down the alley to her front door and she unlocked it and let herself in.

"Thanks," she said.

Then she closed the door. I heard the bolt slide, and turned and headed back to the Olds. When I got in and pulled away the cops blinked their lights once, and then shut them off and settled in to watch.

25

Linda didn't like me staying away overnight. I didn't like it too much myself, but there wasn't much to be done about it. When we had talked about that for most of the late morning, I got to eat some eggs and go to sleep. It was a little after four when I was up again, showered, shaved, smelling like a desert flower and tougher than two armadillos, on my way to the Agony Club to report to my employer.

In the bright sun the parking lot was as empty as it had been last time. I parked again out front under the portcullis and walked in through the door that seemed always slightly ajar. Maybe it was Lippy's trademark, always an open door for a sucker. This time the two gunmen weren't around. Lippy was getting care-less. I walked across the gambling hall and knocked on Lippy's door. No answer. They wouldn't leave the front door open with no one around. I knocked again. Same silence. I turned the knob. The door opened and I went in and found him. Even before I found him I knew what I'd find. The air conditioning had slowed the process, but the smell of death was there when the door opened.

Lippy was in his swivel chair behind his desk, with his back to me. His head hung down, chin on his chest. His hands rested on the arms, stiffened now in death, the fingers beginning to bloat. There was black dried blood mingled with the hair on the back of his head. And mixed with the smell of death was a smell of burnt hair. I looked closely and saw that there was singed hair mingled with the blood. I walked around the desk and squatted in front of Lippy. The exit wound was dark and messy. Lippy's face had begun to bloat.

I stood slowly and looked around the room. No sign of struggle, no sign of robbery. A bottle of good Scotch stood on the sideboard, an ice bucket with water in the bottom, one glass. The file drawers were closed and locked. No sign of any attempt to jimmy them. I went back out into the casino and walked around lightly, feeling the emptiness of the place long before I'd proved it to myself by looking. The two bodyguards were nowhere. Probably in the unemployment office.

I sighed out loud in the empty casino. Maybe I was in the wrong business. Maybe I should be an advance man for a funeral parlor. I walked heavily back into Lippy's office. He must have been sitting comfortably, staring out the window, admiring the desert, and someone had leaned over the desk with a small-caliber handgun and shot him in the back of the head. And I came along and found him. I reached over and picked up Lippy's phone and dialed the cops. Pretty soon, at least, I wouldn't be alone.

A couple of highway patrol guys came roaring in about thirty seconds ahead of a couple of Riverside Sheriff's Deputies, and about two minutes ahead of a cruiser from Poodle Springs which was outside its jurisdiction but showed up anyway. The uniforms milled around and told me not to touch anything and examined the scene of the crime for clues and generally marked time till a couple of Riverside investigators showed up in plain clothes with some lab people and a moonfaced guy from the coroner's office.

A dick named Fox took my statement. He was dark haired and tight skinned and wore his sunglasses pushed up on his head while he talked to me.

"Didn't I see your name on the wire last week?" Fox said. "Discovered a murder victim in Hollywood?"

"It's a gift," I said. "At the peak of the season I sometimes discover two, three corpses a day."

"Maybe you do more than discover them," Fox said.

"Sure," I said. "I blast them for no reason then call the buttons at once and wait around for you to come and suspect me. I love being questioned by cops."

Fox nodded, looking at the notes he'd taken on my statement.

"Cops love it too. We got nothing better to do than talk cute with some second-rate gumshoe from the desert."

"I used to be a second-rate gumshoe from LA.," I said. "I moved out here when I got married."

"Lucky for us," Fox said. "You say Lippy hired you to look for a guy owed him money."

I nodded.

"Who was it?"

I was quiet.

Fox took a deep breath.

"Marlowe," he said, "if you know anything at all besides how to peep through keyholes, you know that this is a murder case and a guy who skipped owing Lippy money is a suspect and that withholding the name of a murder suspect is enough to get your license lifted and your keister in jail."

I nodded. He was right. I was out so far on the limb now for Larry Victor/Les Valentine that I felt like a coconut.

"Guy named Les Valentine," I said. "Lives in the Springs."

Fox turned to one of the Poodle Springs prowlies, an apple-cheeked kid with short blond hair.

"Monson," Fox said, "you know anybody lives in the Springs named Les Valentine?"

Monson nodded and said, "Lemme speak to you alone, Sarge."

Fox raised his eyebrows and followed Monson across the room. They stood near Lippy's door and talked for a few moments in low voices. I got my pipe out while I waited, and packed it, and got it burning. The coroner was through looking at Lippy. Two guys in coveralls came in with a body bag and a dolly. They worked Lippy's stiff body into the bag and wrestled it onto the dolly and went out the office door. Lippy bumped against the door frame on the way out.

Fox and Monson got through talking and Fox came back to me. He threw one leg over the edge of Lippy's desk and looked down at me.

"Monson says Valentine is married to Clayton Blackstone's daughter."

"He had to whisper that?" I said.

"Says you're married to Harlan Potter's daughter."

"That's what he had to whisper?" I said.

"He had to whisper both," Fox said. "He didn't want you to know that us stalwart minions of the law are impressed with stuff like that."

"Are you?" I said.

"Maybe not, but sometimes people up the line are," Fox said.

"Don't worry about Harlan Potter," I said.

"Sure," Fox said. "I won't worry about him, you won't worry about him, the Sheriff, who's up for re-election this fall, won't worry about him. While you're not worrying about him, take a seat out in the casino for a little bit while we clean up here. We might want to chat some more."

I sat in the casino for about an hour and smoked my pipe while technicians cruised around the premises and Fox spent a lot of time talking on the phone in Lippy's office.

At about 7:30 in the evening, Fox came out of Lippy's office.

"We'd like to talk with you a little longer, Marlowe," he said. "We'll go over to the Springs. It's closer."

"I've got my car," I said.

"Monson will ride in with you," Fox said.

26

We were in an interrogation room at the Poodle Springs cop house. I was the special guest. Others included a female stenographer with hair the color of pink grapefruit, Sgt. Whitestone from the Springs, Fox, Lt. Wilton Crump, who was the Riverside County Chief Investigator, and as a surprise treat, Bernie Ohls. Crump was round shouldered and long armed. His neck was short. He had piggy eyes, separated by a wide flat nose. The backs of his hands were hairy. He had on a black suit and vest and a Borsalino hat. He wore the hat tilted back on his head.

"Let's understand each other, Marlowe," Crump said. He was chewing tobacco and holding a paper cup to spit into. "I know you're Harlan Potter's son-in-law and it don't impress me a goddamned bit."

"Oh darn," I said. "I was hoping you'd want to dance with me."

Crump had the tobacco juice cup in his left hand. He reached around under his coat flap with his right hand and came out with a woven leather sap. He showed it to me and smiled, a big mean tobacco-stained smile, and slapped the blackjack softly against his right thigh.

"I don't have much time, Marlowe. I don't have much time for funny, I don't have much time for cute. You found two stiffs in the same week, both shot with a small-caliber gun, in the head. You got something you want to say about that?"

"Just lucky, I guess."

Crump slapped the blackjack again against his thigh and bent toward me. His breath smelled like he might have drunk some Scotch and then eaten Sen-Sen. I could see the red streaking in the whites of his eyes.

"Careful, Marlowe," he said. His voice sounded clotted. "Be goddamned careful."

I gave him a polite smile.

"Now we're just dumb coppers," Crump said, still close to my face, "and so a smart rich private eye like you probably knows stuff that we don't see."

"I'm not rich," I said. "My wife's rich."

Crump talked on as if I hadn't spoken.

"But we were wondering if there might not be some sort of connection, maybe, between the two stiffs you found. And maybe even that you might be telling the L.A. coppers one thing, and us another thing. Lieutenant Ohls here was wondering that enough to drive all the way out here after we called him and said we'd been talking to you."

Ohls was leaning against the wall across the room, with his hat tilted forward over his eyes and his arms folded across his chest.

"We might be wondering, too, before Crump frightens us both to death, if you might care to talk a little about how come you were chasing around Western and Sunset at three-thirty in the a.m. with Angel Victor, who is, for the record, the wife of the chief suspect in the murder of Lola Faithful."

"If he don't give me an answer I like," Crump said, "I'll do a hell of a lot more than frighten him." He glanced over at Ohls and then glared in my face.

I said to Bernie, "If you can get Buzzard Breath, here, out of my face, maybe we can talk."

Still leaning in close to me, Crump hit me on the side of the left knee with the blackjack. The pain ran the length of my leg both ways and into my groin. The leg started to throb immediately. There was a hint of tobacco juice at the corner of Crump's mouth.

He snarled at me, "Buzzard Breath, Smart Boy?"

Still leaning on the wall with his arms folded, Ohls said, "Put the sap away, Crump."

Crump straightened and stared across at Ohls.

"The hell with you," he said. "He's my prisoner."

Ohls took out one of his little cigars and put it in his mouth and got it lit. Then he straightened from the wall and walked easily across the room and stood directly in front of Crump with his face maybe a half inch away from Crump's. He let a little smoke drift out as he spoke.

"You either put the sap away," Ohls said in a soft and pleasant voice, "or I will strain it through your teeth."

Crump jerked a little, as if someone had jabbed him. No one said anything for a moment. The two men stood close together.

Then Crump said, "Aw, the hell with this," and stuffed the sap in his back pocket and turned and left the room. Ohls smiled as if at some private joke and turned and went back and leaned on the wall.

"Whyn't you talk about all this, Marlowe, take your time," he said. "We got all night. Fox here can represent Riverside."

I got out a cigarette and lit it and took in some smoke. Maybe it was time to dump this thing, to tell them the thing they didn't know and let them run with it and go home and drink gimlets with my wife. When they knew that Les owed Lippy dough, and that Les was also Larry, the one Lola had argued with before she ended up dead in his office, then the whole thing would go away. Larry would be gone and Muriel would be alone and Angel, with her big eyes and her smile . . .

"Lippy always had a couple of Roscoes with him," I said. "Whoever murdered him had to get around them first."

Ohls didn't move, or speak.

"I'd guess a woman," I said. "Small gun, whoever did it got close to him. He had his back turned. Scotch was out as if there was going to be a drink. But only one glass. Maybe he had a romantic rendezvous that went bang in the night."

Ohls took his hat off and held it down by his side, holding it by the brim. He had the little cigar in his mouth and he spoke around it.

"We've done this before, Marlowe. We can guess that sort of stuff without you."

I shrugged. "It's all I've got, Bernie."

Ohls tapped the hat against his thigh softly, took the cigar out of his mouth with his other hand, dislodged a bit of tobacco from under his upper lip with his tongue and spit the tobacco delicately toward the corner.

"You discover two homicides in a week," Ohls said. "That could be a coincidence. But in thirty-two years of police work I've never seen a coincidence like that."

There didn't seem much worth saying to that. I let it pass.

"Coincidences don't do anything for us, Marlowe. They don't take us anywhere. Believing in coincidences is believing in dead ends. Cops hate dead ends, Marlowe."

"I know," I said. "I worry about that. Some nights I can't sleep."

"Not only do you find two stiffs in a week, but you do so in the course of looking for a deadbeat named Les Valentine, who, it turns out, is Clayton Blackstone's son-in-law."

"And Clayton Blackstone worries you?"

"Yeah, I stay up nights too," Ohls said. He walked over to one of the scarred maple desks and put his cigar out in a half-empty paper cup of coffee. He turned back toward me.

"You got no client, Marlowe. You got nobody to protect. Unless you're protecting yourself."

"There's nothing more I can tell you, Bernie," I said.

"Maybe you shoulda let Crump have him, Lieutenant," Fox said.

"Crump is a thug with a badge," Ohls said. "I don't like him."

We were all quiet then. The pink-haired stenographer was poised and ready to record more. Except there wasn't any more.

Ohls sighed. "Okay, Marlowe," he said. He turned to Sgt. Whitestone. "Use your jail?"

"Sure," Whitestone said.

"Book him," Ohls said. "Stick him in a cell. Maybe a connection will occur to him."

"What charge, Lieutenant?"

"Your choice," Ohls said. "You'll think of something."

Then he put on his hat and walked out of the room.

27

It was quiet in the Poodle Springs hoosegow. There were a couple of other prisoners, but it was late and they were asleep. The only noise was the sound of sleeping men, an occasional snore, a mutter, once a brief sob.

I lay on the bunk in the dark. Outside the late night life of the Springs went on. People had midnight snacks and made love and watched movies on TV and slept quietly with the dog at the foot of the bed and the refrigerator humming quietly in the kitchen. The jail was attached to the police station and I could hear the patrol cars come and go: the sound of their radios, indistinct in the night, the crunch of tires on gravel, once the siren as a car pulled out in a hurry. But mostly there was nothing to hear, and nothing to do.

I wondered if Lippy would have been killed if I'd told the cops all I knew. If I'd told them even as much as I'd told Blackstone. Guys like Lippy were always walking on the railing, but dying's a long fall. Blackstone had no reason to kill Lippy, even if he found out that he was chasing Les for money. A word from the boss would have been enough. But Les had a reason, and he had a reason to kill Lola Faithful too, a blackmail reason having to do with a picture. Whoever killed Lola had also cleaned out Larry's files—I smiled to myself in the dark. When he was in Poodle Springs I called him Les, when he was in L.A. I called him Larry. No wonder I was confused—were they looking for the picture? Why would the killer take all the files? Because he was looking for something, or she was, and he didn't have time to look through them all. If Larry killed her he'd know what was in the files. He wouldn't have to take them. But he might because he'd know the cops would find them and maybe he didn't want them known, though there were pictures on sale at any newsstand as graphic as Larry's. Still, he might be embarrassed.

The turnkey strolled down the corridor outside the row of cells, his crepe-soled shoes squeaking. He paused in front of each cell and stared in for a moment before he moved on.

There hadn't been anyone in all those nude photos that I recognized except Sondra Lee. And I had her picture tucked under the floor mat in the trunk of my car. Suppose Larry had agreed to pay Lola blackmail and she came and brought the picture and he killed her and took it. He'd destroy the picture—but would Lola show up with the only print? Would she be that stupid? I didn't believe it. Blackmailers don't give up their leverage that easy. Even stupid blackmailers.

I thought about a cigarette. I didn't have any, or my pipe, or for that matter my shoelaces or my tie or my belt. I got up and walked in a tight circle around the cell a few times. It didn't make me sleepy. I lay back down on the bunk. There was no sheet, but there was a mattress and a blanket. I'd been in jails that had neither. Ah, Marlowe, you glamorous adventurer. Why the hell wasn't it Larry? Even if he did have a pretty, big-eyed little wife who adored him. Was she the legal one? Maybe I should check the bigamy laws when I got out. Hadn't had a lot of bigamy cases lately.

I did some deep breathing.

And where was the picture? Lola would have kept a copy. It wasn't in her house. If the cops had found it, it would have led them somewhere. They were as stuck as I was, stucker because they didn't know the things that I was stuck about. Could be in a safe-deposit box. Except where was the key? And whiskey-voiced old broads like Lola didn't usually keep safe-deposit boxes. Maybe she stashed the negative with a friend. Except whiskey-voiced old broads like Lola didn't usually trust friends with valuable property. The simplest answer was Larry again, and the simplest answer on Lippy was Les. And Les was Larry.

I did some more deep breathing.

Somewhere before morning I dozed off finally and dreamed that I was in love with a huge nude photograph of Linda, and every time I reached it Tweedledum and Tweedledee grabbed it away and ran off in perfect tandem.

28

At six A.M. they brought me some warm coffee and a stale roll. I sat on the bunk and ate. My head ached, my knee throbbed steadily. I touched the spot where Crump had hit me. It was puffy and sore. My stomach felt uneasy as I drank the coffee. I'd had maybe two hours' sleep.

At 10:30 A.M. a new turnkey came on down the corridor and stopped in front of my cell.

"Okay, Marlowe," he said. "You're sprung."

I got up stiffly and limped after him as we went along the corridor and up three stairs and into the lobby of the cop house. Linda was there, and a guy in a white suit and a loud shirt.

The guy in the loud shirt said, "Mr. Marlowe, Harry Simpson. Sorry we took so long. I had to wait until court opened this morning to get a writ."

He had a dark tan and shiny black loafers with a little gold chain across the tongue of each. His shirt was open halfway to the navel and his bare chest looked like a leather washboard. The hair on his chest was grey. He had a little thick moustache and his wiry hair was tinged with more grey. He wore a pinky ring. A Poodle Springs lawyer. In a little while he'd be calling me baby.

Linda stood behind him; she didn't speak. Her eyes rested on me so heavily I could almost feel the weight of her look. I got my stuff back, signed a receipt, and we went out the front door. No alarms sounded. Linda's Cadillac was parked in the *No Parking, Police Only* spot beside a Mercedes convertible with the top down that I knew had to belong to my attorney.

"Where's your car?" Linda said.

"Out back," I said.

"I'll drive you home and send Tino back to get it," Linda said. "You look awful."

But better than I felt.

Simpson said, "You may have to appear, Mr. Marlowe. I'll try to squelch it, and, frankly, Mr. Potter's name carries some weight, but I can't guarantee anything."

"More than mine does," I said.

Linda opened the passenger side of the Cadillac.

"Get in, darling," she said.

"Anything I should tell your dad?" Simpson said.

"Tell him thanks," Linda said. "I'll call him later."

Then she went around and got in and we drove home in silence.

When we got home Linda said, "I think you should shower and get some sleep. We can talk later."

I was too tired to debate that, or much else. I did as she suggested, though I reversed the order.

At six o'clock that evening I was nearly human again. I had showered and shaved and was sitting by the pool in a silk robe with an ice pack on my swollen knee. Tino brought me a double vodka gimlet on the rocks, and a single for Madame. The gimlet was the color of straw and limpid as I looked at it in the thick square glass. The water in the pool moved slightly in the easy breeze that had come with the evening. I dipped into the gimlet and felt the drink ease into me and along the nerve trails. I looked at Linda. She was sitting on the chaise, her feet on the floor, her knees together, bent forward a little with her hands in her lap, both hands folded around her glass.

"Daddy's furious," she said.

"The hell with him," I said.

"He got you out," she said.

"The hell with him anyway," I said. "How are you?"

She shook her head slowly and stared down into her glass as if, in the bottom, was an answer she didn't quite have.

"I've been in the jug before, Linda. It's an occupational hazard, like boredom and sore feet."

"The police said you were obstructing justice."

"The police say what they need to say," I said. "They wanted me to tell them something I didn't think they should know."

"And they put you in jail? Is that legal?"

"Probably not, but it happens all the time. After a while you get to understand it."

"Is it legal not to tell them what they want to know?"

"Same answer, I guess. You can't do my work and keep your self-respect if you let the cops decide what you should do."

"I frankly fail to see how you can do your work and keep your self-respect," Linda said.

"Because it involves spending time occasionally in jail? Because it brings you into contact with the lower classes?"

"Damn it, Philip, that's not fair," Linda said. "It's not my fault my father's rich."

"No," I said, "it isn't. And it isn't mine either. But one thing you can count on, you don't get as rich as Harlan Potter in this country without cutting some corners, and breaking some rules, and spending time with people you wouldn't care to break a crumpet with."

Linda shook her head fast several times.

"I don't know about that. I don't even care about that. What I know is that this is no kind of marriage I understand. You're out all night half the time. I don't know where you are or what you're doing. You might be getting killed. I wake up in the morning and get a call saying you're in jail. My husband. Here? In the Springs? In jail?"

"What will they say at lunch?" I said.

"Damn it, don't be so poor-snob high and mighty, Marlowe. These are my friends. I care about them. I want them to care about you. I don't want to know that they're laughing behind my back at my husband."

"They'll do that anyway," I said. "Not because I'm a gumshoe. Not because I spent the night in jail. They'll laugh at me because I'm a failure. I don't have any money. In this great Republic that's how the judgment is made, darling."

"But I have money, I have enough money for both of us."

"Which is why, as I keep trying to explain, I can't

take it. The way I keep from being a failure is to be free. To be my absolute own man. Me, Marlowe, the Galahad of the gutter. I decide what I'll do. I won't be bought, or pushed, not even by love. You're a success if you have money, but you give up too much."

It was a long speech for me. I washed it down with some gimlet. It didn't help. Gimlets were for early afternoons in quiet bars where the tables gleamed with polish and the light filtered through the bottles and the bartender had a crisp white shirt with the cuffs turned back. Gimlets were for holding hands across the table and saying nothing and knowing everything. I put the drink on the table. Linda hadn't touched hers; she used it to stare into.

"When you're home," Linda said in a flat voice, "and we go to bed, there's a gun on the bureau, beside your wallet and car keys."

"I used to sleep with it in my teeth," I said. "But I figured it was safer out here in the desert."

Linda looked up from her gimlet and stared at me for a moment.

"This isn't working," she said finally. Then she stood, still holding the gimlet in both hands. "I'm not saying it's your fault . . . but it isn't working."

She turned and walked back into the house.

I picked up the nearly full double gimlet and stared

at it for a little while without drinking, then I flicked my wrist and sluiced the contents in a thin arc onto the ground and carefully put the empty glass upside down on the table and leaned back on the chaise and listened to the ice melt in the bag on my knee.

29

I spent the night in the guest room. In the morning I was out of the house early. I got coffee in a place on Riverside that also sold stuffed burros, and little key chains with genuine gold nuggets attached. The desert looked harsher than I'd ever seen it as I drove over to Muriel Valentine's house. The earth had a harsh eroded look like an angry dowager, and the cactus plants seemed more loutish than I remembered them yesterday. The hard disinterested sky was cloudless and the heat was dry and unyielding as I got out and walked up Muriel's walk again. The houseboy answered my ring and let me stand in the hall while he went to fetch Mrs. Valentine.

When she appeared she seemed as bleak as the desert. Her eyes looked as if she'd cried and her mouth was thin. "He's not here," she said.

"Your husband," I said.

"Yes. I don't know where he is."

The tip of her tongue appeared and touched her lower lip and disappeared.

"When did he leave?"

"He's been gone since the day after you left him here," she said.

"You know Lipshultz is dead," I said.

"Yes."

"Did you know he worked for your father?" I said.

She stepped back as if I had poked a live snake at her.

"Your father owns the Agony Club," I said.

She didn't say anything. She kept looking at me, her face tight, the tip of her tongue darting occasionally out over her lower lip. I looked back at her. Nothing else happened. Finally I turned and walked out and closed the door behind me. She felt worse than I did. I got in the Olds and sat for a moment staring at nothing, then I put the Olds in gear and headed for L.A.

I found Angel sitting on her front porch looking at the beach. There was toast grown cold on a saucer and a cup of tea turned dark with the tea bag sitting in it.

Angel sat in the rocker with her knees up, her arms around them, her chin resting on them. The rocker shifted slightly but she wasn't really rocking.

"He's not here," she said.

"You waiting for him?" I said.

"Yes. I didn't go to work. I can't. I have to be here in case he comes."

"I've lost him," I said. "He's not where I left him."

The rocker moved a little. Angel didn't say anything.

The sound of the surf, muffled as it rolled over the sand, was a white sound behind us. There were people on the beach moving past us in both directions. Up the beach a bulldozer was moving sand around near a new playground.

"He's not worth this, Angel," I said. "He's got no spine."

"I love him," she said and shrugged. The rocker moved a little again and then stopped.

I thought about Muriel, her face scraped bare of anything but hurt. I looked at Angel. Would Angel forgive that too, another woman. Hell, another wife. This creep had two wives crazy about him. I was on my way to having none. "You wouldn't have a guess where he might be?" I said.

She shook her head.

"He'll come back here, though," she said. "Sooner or later."

"I'm not so sure, Angel," I said, "that he didn't kill Lippy."

"He wouldn't," she said.

"And if he killed Lippy he might have killed Lola."

Angel simply shook her head, grimly, and stared at the beach.

There wasn't anything else to say. If he'd killed Lola and I'd helped him get away then I was on the hook for Lippy as much as he was. I tried a wry smile at her and turned and went away from there. When I glanced back she was still staring at the beach, motionless.

I drove from Venice downtown to see Bernie Ohls. He was in his cubicle. Empty desk with a phone on it, swivel chair, hat on a hook on the back of the door.

"Harlan Potter spring you?" he said when I came in. "Or you tunnel out of the Springs jail?"

"Potter," I said.

"Bet he and his daughter were happy about that," Ohls said.

"Like spawning salmon," I said. I sat in the plain chair opposite the desk. There were no pictures on the walls, no citation, not even a window. Ohls had killed at least nine men that I knew of, several when they thought he was covered.

The office was as blank as a waiter's stare.

"You're not looking too good, Marlowe," Ohls said. "You look like a man who didn't sleep well, who had a lousy breakfast."

"Les Valentine and Larry Victor are the same guy," I said.

Ohls was sitting with one foot cocked on the open lower drawer of his desk. He took his foot off the drawer and swiveled the chair around and slowly placed both feet on the ground.

"Is that a fact?" he said. I could see him turning this over in his mind.

"Aren't they both married?" Ohls said.

"Yeah."

"You've known this for a while."

"I've known it since before Lola Faithful got killed," I said.

"You said something to us, maybe Lipshultz wouldn't have gone down," Ohls said.

"Yeah."

Ohls shifted his seat around and put one foot back up on the open drawer. He clasped both hands behind his neck.

"Marlowe of the desert," he said. "Hawkshaw to the stars."

I let that pass. I'd earned what was coming.

"You think that maybe you played it a little too tight this time, cutie? And a guy gets buzzed that didn't have to? Say Lippy deserved it more than some. He didn't deserve it this time, from this guy."

"Nobody deserves it, Bernie."

"Sure, Marlowe, let your heart bleed a little. And while you're at it why don't you explain to me why you held out on us."

"I didn't think he did it," I said.

"You didn't think he did it," Ohls said. "Who appointed you? This is cop business, friend."

"He's a loser, he's a spineless creep, but he's got a nice little girl who loves everything about him."

"Only one?" Ohls said.

I shrugged. "I'll get to that. I still don't know if he did it, but I have to admit he looks more likely every time you turn it around."

"You covered for some guy you barely know because he's got a nice wife."

"They looked happy, Bernie. You don't see too much of that. And I figured if you got him you'd like him for it so much he'd be in Q before the public defender got his briefcase open."

"I don't railroad people, Marlowe."

"Sure you don't, Bernie, and you don't turn down a likely suspect either. This guy had argued with the victim earlier, he's got to have a shaky record. He's got the gumption of a popsicle . . ." I turned my palms up and spread my hands.

"Bartender says the beef with Lola started when she showed him a picture. You know anything about that?"

"Larry had a file full of nude photos," I said. "I checked the files when I found his office."

"They're not there now," Ohls said. "Nude pictures of who?"

"Women, explicit, kind of stuff worth some money twenty-five years ago."

"Not much of a living in it now," Ohls said. "Unless you want it for blackmail."

I shrugged.

"Okay, Marlowe," Ohls said, "you can tell me everything, from the beginning real slow, lotta small words, so as not to confuse me. And once I've heard it all, and I'm satisfied that you're not being cute, then we'll have a stenographer in and we'll go through it all for her."

He put both feet up on his desk and leaned farther back in his chair, his hands laced across his solar plexus.

"Go," he said.

I told him pretty much everything, leaving out the fact that I had a picture of Sondra Lee in the trunk of my car. When I came to the part about Blackstone, Ohls whistled silently to himself. When I was finished he said, "And you still think Larry, Les, whatever the hell his name is, didn't do it?"

"I don't know, Bernie. I'm here. I've told you what I know. You and I both know how long this guy will be around if Clayton Blackstone finds out his daughter's married to a bigamist."

"A little work for fast Eddie," Ohls said.

"Damn little," I said.

"We could charge you with obstructing justice," Ohls said. "Interfering with an officer in the performance of his duty, aiding and abetting the escape of a felon, accessory after the fact of homicide, obtaining motor vehicle information dishonestly, impersonating a police officer and being stupider than three sheep."

"I got an overdue library book, too," I said. "May as well make a clean breast of it."

"Get out of here," Ohls said.

"What about the stenographer?" I said.

"The hell with the stenographer," Ohls said. "If you so much as walk on a posted lawn, Marlowe . . ." He waved his hand, dismissing me with the back of it. The way a man shoos away a gnat.

I got up and went.

30

Movement is sometimes an adequate substitute for action. I had nothing else to do, and no one else to see, so I drove out to West L.A. looking for Sondra Lee. The blond receptionist with the long thighs was there again. She told me that Sondra Lee was expected in the next half hour, and I sat on one of the silver tweed couches with no arms that curved along the left wall of the office. On the walls, in silver frames, were fashion shots of their clients, black and white theatrically lit, with the archness that only fashion photographers can capture. Sondra was one of them, in profile, gazing into some ethereal beyond, wearing an enormous black and white hat. Which was much more than she was wearing in the picture I had rolled up in my pocket.

Time edged past like a clumsy inchworm. A tall, thin, overdressed woman came in and picked up some messages from the receptionist and went back out. Another woman, raven hair, pale skin, carmine lipstick, came in and spoke to the receptionist and passed on into one of the inner offices. I looked around, spotted an ashtray on a silver pedestal, dragged it close to me, got out a cigarette and lit it. I dropped the empty match into the ashtray and took in some smoke. There was a big clock shaped like a banjo on the wall back of the receptionist. It ticked so softly it took me a while to hear it. Occasionally the phone made a soft murmur and the receptionist said brightly, "Triton Agency, good afternoon." While I was there she said it maybe 40 times, without variation. My cigarette was down to the stub. I put it out in the ashtray and arched my back, and while I was arching it in came Sondra Lee. She was wearing a little yellow dress and a big yellow hat. She didn't recognize me, even when I stood up and said, "Miss Lee."

She turned her head with that impersonal friendly look that people get who are used to being recognized.

"Marlowe," I said. "We had a talk at your home the other day about Les Valentine, among other things."

The smile stayed just as impersonal, but it got less friendly.

"And?" she said.

"And we had such fun that I wanted to talk a little longer."

"I'm sorry, Mr. Marlowe, I'm afraid I can't. I have a shoot this afternoon."

I walked across to her, and as I went I took the naked picture of her from my inside pocket and unrolled it. I held it so that she could see and the receptionist couldn't.

"Just a few moments," I said. "I thought you might be able to help me with this picture."

She looked at it, and her face showed nothing.

"Oh, all right," she said. "We can talk in here."

She led me into a small dressing room with a big mirror ringed with lights. There was a make-up table full of jars and tubes and powders and brushes, a stool in front of it, a daybed against the wall to the right of the door, and a tall director's chair. On the back of the black canvas was written *Sondra* in white script. She sat in the chair, her long legs carelessly stretched in front of her.

"So you are just another little nasty blackmailer," she said evenly.

"I'm not so little," I said.

"For your information, you roach, I'll give you exactly nothing for those pictures. That's what they're worth. Send them to the magazines, post them in the bus terminal, I don't care. It's thirty years past the time when pictures like that could hurt me."

"So they weren't much good to Larry Victor," I said.

"No more than they are to you, cheapie," she said. She took out a pastel filtered cigarette and put it in her mouth and lit it with a transparent lighter that showed you how much fluid was left.

"But he tried," I said.

"Sure he tried, don't all the scum balls try?"

"And you told him to breeze," I said.

"Tommy did," she said.

"And maybe you put a little something behind it," I said.

Sondra shrugged. "You're lucky Tommy's not here now," she said.

"Yeah," I said. "I barely escaped with my life last time."

Her face said she didn't remember too much about last time.

"I was at your house," I said, "asking you about a photographer named Les Valentine."

"I was on a toot," she said.

"Yeah. You suggested, as I recall, that I might want to toot along with you."

If she remembered she didn't show it. There was no sign of embarrassment.

"Tommy hates that," she said. She didn't sound like she cared if Tommy hated that or not. "So what do you want, Marlowe? Or are you one of those guys gets his rocks off talking to a woman while you look at her nude picture?"

"That's one of my favorites," I said. "But this time I'm trying to get a handle on Larry Victor."

She cocked her head and looked at me for a moment.

"Larry? How come?"

"Case I'm working on," I said.

"You're not trying to shake me down?"

"I wouldn't dare," I said. "What can you tell me about Larry?"

"A full-fledged creepster," Sondra said. "Took third-rate pictures and couldn't make a living except doing nudes for skin magazines and adult bookstores. He shot a lot of us when we were new, trying to make a living, trying to get noticed. He had a nice line, scored a lot of the models. God knows why—he wore a toupee and his hands sweated all the time. But . . ." She shrugged. "Takes all kinds."

"And he'd keep prints and if you got to be an important model," I said, "he'd try to blackmail you."

"Or if you got into pictures," she said. "Studios were always worried about that stuff. Kids that got into pictures probably did pay off."

"Not a bad racket, then. Sells the product once and in some cases sells it again for more, later."

"Like a growth stock," Sondra said. She smiled and took a drag on her cigarette and held the smoke for a long moment, then let it slide out through the smile. "Only times changed. Pretty soon no one much cared if you showed your tush in public and Larry's business took a nosedive."

"Outmoded by changing times," I said, "like livery stables. Did you know he'd gotten married?"

"I lost track of Larry a while back, as soon as I climbed out of the gutter he works in."

"And you don't know a photographer named Les Valentine?"

"No."

"Muriel Valentine? Muriel Blackstone? Angel Victor?" As I did the names, Sondra kept shaking her head.

"Any close friends from the old days you'd remember?" I said.

She laughed shortly. "Friends? Not that you'd notice. If the little creep had any friends they were likely to be women." She shook her head again. "I never understood that," she said.

"You can't remember any names?" I said.

She dragged in some more smoke and blew it out in a big puff. She shook her head.

"No," she said, "I can't."

"And you wouldn't have a guess where he might be now?"

"Is that it?" she said. "He's missing?"

I nodded.

"No," she said. "No. I'd have no idea."

I was still holding her picture. I gave it to her. She took it and looked at it.

"I was a piece of work in those days," she said.

"Still are," I said.

She smiled at me. "Thanks," she said. I turned toward the door.

"Marlowe," she said.

I stopped with one hand on the doorknob and turned to look at her.

"I remember every detail of what happened when you visited me last time," she said.

"Me too," I said.

She smiled at me. "The offer still holds," she said.

"Thanks," I said and gave her my killer grin and left.

31

I went back up Westwood to the Village and then onto Weyburn and up Hilgard past UCLA to Sunset and drove east.

I barely knew Larry Victor and I was getting very sick of him already. My marriage was in trouble, the cops were in a contest to see who had the best plan for locking me up the longest, Clayton Blackstone and Eddie Garcia were lurking in the corners and everything I learned about Larry Victor made me wonder why I was taking any trouble for him at all. Maybe he had killed Lola, maybe he was stupid enough to kill her in his office. Maybe he killed Lippy too, maybe he was tougher than I thought he was. If a guy was stupid

enough to kill a woman in his own office after recently
arguing with her in public, was he smart enough to
get the two bodyguards out of the way in order to kill
Lippy while they had a drink and Lippy looked out
the window?

I passed the pink stucco silliness of the Beverly Hills
Hotel, half hidden by palm trees. On both sides of Sunset were big homes, expensive and ugly in that special
way that Southern California money finds to combine
both. Movie stars, directors, producers, agents, people
who had found a way to package emptiness and sell it
as dreams.

Lola had to have been blackmailing Larry, with a
picture. And she wouldn't have been so dumb as to go
to the meeting with her only copy. She must have had
a back-up. So where was it? I had tossed her house like
a Caesar salad and found nothing. Not a crouton. So
where would she hide it? Where would I hide something like that?

I was on the strip now, billboards of singers I'd never
heard of, boutiques dickied up to look like French country cottages. At Horn Ave a guy with long curly black
hair turned onto Sunset driving a two-seater sports car
that was longer than my Olds. He squealed rubber as
he floored it for fifty yards before he had to brake for
a stoplight. The car was ugly, impractical, ostentatious,

uneconomical and badly designed for city driving, but it was expensive.

I drove on through Hollywood and swung up Kenmore to Lola's house. I had a thought.

The lawn looked a little more unkempt, but everything else seemed the same. People die, hearts break, dynasties fall on their kisser, and the grass keeps growing a little at a time, and the fronts of houses weather very slowly. I parked out front and walked up the front steps and stood under the cooling overhang. The mailbox was stuffed with mail that Lola would never read; some catalogues and advertising flyers had collected on the floor under the mailbox. Clearly no one had notified the post office. I took the envelopes out of the mailbox. Most of them were bills; there was nothing personal among them. I opened the door again the same way I had last time and went in, again. It was as I had left it. I put the mail on the hall table and looked around the house. Last time I'd been looking for a picture. This time I was looking for something else, a key, a receipt, something to tell me where she hid the picture. It had to be there. And it was. After an hour I found it. In among the unpaid bills stuffed into a pigeonhole in the old desk in her den was a receipt from the parcel room at Union Station.

It took me half an hour to get to Union Station and

park and find the checked-luggage office and present my receipt. A black man of many years shuffled back into the catacombs of storage and emerged after maybe three weeks with a flat manila envelope sealed with transparent tape along the flap. *Lola Faithful* was scrawled in a big flowery hand across the face of the envelope. The *i* in *Faithful* was dotted with a big circle. I took the envelope and went and sat in the waiting room on an empty bench and opened the envelope. There was an 8 × 10 glossy, and a small glassine envelope with a negative. The glossy was a picture of Muriel Blackstone Valentine wearing high-heeled leather boots and nothing else. Naked, the body was all it promised to be. She was smiling a seductive smile that was skewed a little and her eyes were glassy. I held the negative up and looked at it against the light. It matched. I put the negative and the print back in the manila envelope and headed out under the arches, past the cab stand toward where I'd parked my car.

32

I was back in Venice, where Angel worked as a waitress at a combination café and bookstore on the beach. The lunch crowd was gone and there were only a few early lush types sipping drinks at the outdoor tables and trying to look as if one would do them, they were just passing time. I sat and ordered coffee. Angel brought it to me.

"Take a minute," I said. "I need to show you something."

I pushed a chair away from the table with my foot.

"They don't allow me to sit with the customers," Angel said, "but I'm due for my break. You can come in back."

I got up and followed her through the kitchen to a storage room where full gallon-size cans of tomatoes and jugs of olive oil were stacked against the bare cinder-block walls. There was a mop and bucket next to the door.

I took the picture of Muriel out and handed it to Angel.

"You know her?" I said.

Angel shook her head. Her cheeks colored. I'd been looking at so many nude pictures lately I'd forgotten that she might be embarrassed. I liked her for it.

"Sorry," I said. "But it's the only picture I've got."

"It's all right," Angel said. She looked at the picture again. "She does have a wonderful body," she said.

"Sure," I said. "Larry took this picture."

"Larry?"

"I can't prove it, but I know it's the picture that Lola showed to Larry when they had their fight. She was trying to blackmail him with it."

"Because he took a naked picture?"

"Because it's his wife," I said.

Angel smiled tentatively at me.

"I don't understand," she said.

"Larry also goes by the name Les Valentine," I said. "Under that name he is married to this woman, Muriel Blackstone, now Muriel Valentine."

"Larry's married to me," Angel said.

"Yes," I said, "and Les is married to her and Les and Larry are the same guy."

"I don't believe that," Angel said.

"No reason you should," I said. "But it's the truth and I've kept it from you as long as I'm going to."

"I don't know why you come to me and lie to me like this," Angel said. "You must be very evil or very sick."

"Tired," I said. "Tired of wading around in this swamp. Maybe your husband did kill somebody, maybe he didn't; but he's bolted again and I don't know where he is and I don't care. No more secrets."

"You still don't know where Larry is?" Angel said. It was as if everything else I'd told her had washed off her without a mark.

"No," I said. "Do you?"

"No. Do you think something happened to him?"

"No, I think he did what he knows how to do. He ran away."

"He wouldn't leave me," Angel said.

I just shook my head. I didn't know what the hell Larry/Les would do or where he'd go, and I was beginning to doubt that I ever would.

"He wouldn't," Angel said again.

I fished a card out of my wallet and handed it to her.

"If you find out where he is," I said, "you can call me."

She took the card without looking at it. I doubted that she'd call. I doubted that anyone would call. Ever.

I went out of the restaurant and back along the beach. The Pacific lumbered in toward me. The swells looked tired as they crested and fell apart on the beach, and gathered themselves and withdrew slowly, and got upright and fell toward the beach again.

Time to go back to the Springs.

33

Linda was pacing in the living room past the Hammond organ built into the bar, past the glass wall with the butterflies and back, past the oversized fireplace. The nude picture of Muriel Blackstone was on the bar. Nobody was looking at it.

"I admit I am astonished," Linda said. "I had no idea that Muffy Blackstone . . ." She shook her head.

"Maybe most women lead lives of quiet desperation, too," I said.

"Maybe they do, but I must say I don't see why my husband has to be the one to dig that up. I mean, really, Philip," she nodded at the picture, "aren't you embarrassed?"

"It's been a long time," I said, "since I got embarrassed."

"Well, you should be. I am."

"I'm a detective, lady. You knew that when you married me."

"I guess I didn't think you'd always be a detective."

"Or you thought I'd grow a thin moustache and drink port and figure out who killed Mrs. Posselthwait's cousin Sue Sue in Count Boslewick's castle garden, without ever getting bark mulch on my shoes," I said. "And maybe we'd dine occasionally with an amusing inspector of police."

"Damn you, Marlowe, can't you see how it is for me? Can't you budge even a little bit?"

"Depends what you need me to budge on," I said. "I can budge on where we live, or who we entertain, or where we go for our honeymoon. But you want me to budge on who I am. On what I am. And I can't. This is what I am, a guy who ends up with dirty pictures in his possession."

"And two murders," Linda said, "and some story about bigamy?"

"And murder and bigamy, and probably a lot worse to come," I said. "It's the way I make my living. It's the way I got to be the guy you wanted to marry in the first place."

"And if I were poor?"

"You're not poor. I'm poor and you're not," I said. "There's no point talking about things that aren't so."

"What are you going to do with that picture of Muffy?" Linda said.

"I don't know," I said. "I didn't understand this case before and now I understand it a lot less."

Linda stepped to the bar and picked up the picture.

"I could tear it up right now," she said.

"Sure," I said, "but I've made copies."

"You think of everything, don't you," she said.

"Everything that doesn't matter," I said. "I haven't thought of who killed Lola Faithful or Lippy. I haven't thought of where Les Valentine is. I haven't thought of a way to keep the cops from tearing up my license, which I don't have copies made of."

Linda dropped the picture back on the bar.

"Perhaps she had Les take it, you know, just for them," she said.

"Maybe."

"Darling," Linda said, "let's go to Mexico again. Today, right now. I could be packed in an hour."

"You could be packed in two," I said. "And you'd pay for the trip and when we got back I'd still have to make a living."

"Damn you," Linda said. "Goddamn you." She

walked to the picture window that looked out onto the patio and pressed her forehead against it.

"I'm embarrassed with my friends about what you're doing. Can you imagine the talk at the club when I had to get you out of jail? I'm terrified when you're not home and I'm humiliated when there are social occasions and I have to go alone, and I don't even know where you are."

There was nothing to be said. So I said it.

"I know it seems so terribly snobbish and petty to you," Linda said. Her forehead was still against the glass. "But it is my life, the only one I've known. And my life matters to me too."

"I know," I said.

She turned from the window and stared at me.

"So what are we to do?" she said.

"You have to live your life," I said. "I have to live mine."

"And we can't seem to do that together," Linda said.

"No, we can't seem to," I said.

We were silent for a long time.

"I'll ask my attorney to draw up divorce papers," Linda said finally. "I want you to have something."

"No," I said. "I'll never touch it. It's not mine."

"I know," Linda said.

We were silent again. Through the plate glass two swallows darted into the bougainvillaea and disappeared in the leaves.

"I'll stay in the guest room tonight," I said. "Tomorrow I'll move back to L.A."

She nodded. There were tears on her face.

"Damn it, Marlowe," she said. "We love each other."

"I know," I said. "It's what makes it so hard."

34

I found a furnished apartment in front on Ivar north of the boulevard, in a stucco building built around a courtyard in the days when Hollywood had more screen stars and fewer hookers. My old office in the Cahuenga Building was still empty, so I moved back in. The desk, the two file cabinets, the old calendar remained, the outer office was still empty. Two dead flies lay on the floor just inside the door that still said *Philip Marlowe, Investigation*. I put a fresh bottle of bourbon in the bottom drawer and rinsed out the two glasses on the sink in the corner, and I was ready for business.

Except there wasn't any business. A cousin to the dead flies in the outer office was buzzing lethargically against the window pane behind my desk. I put my feet up on the desk. The fly paused in his buzzing and looked at the impenetrable transparent space before him. He rubbed his face with his front feet, then buzzed again, but there wasn't much pizzazz in the buzz. It was a losing battle. He rattled for a minute against the window pane, then settled back down to the sill again and stood with his legs spraddled. I got up and carefully opened the window. The fly stayed motionless for a time, then he buzzed once and soared lazily out through the window and into the traffic fumes, three stories above Hollywood Boulevard. And then he was gone. I closed the window and sat back down. No one came in, no one called. No one cared if I got rabies or went to Paris.

At noon I went out and got a ham sandwich and some coffee at a joint on the boulevard and went back to my office to try sitting with my feet on the other corner. I still had my naked pictures of Muffy in the middle drawer of my desk. I still didn't know what to do with them. The negative was locked in the old floor safe behind the inner office door. I still didn't know where Les/Larry was and I didn't have a client.

I heard the outer door open and shut. And then Eddie Garcia came into my office and glanced around once and stepped aside and Clayton Blackstone came in behind him. Eddie went over and leaned blankly against one of the file cabinets. Blackstone sat down in my client chair. He had on a double-breasted grey pinstripe that cost more than my car.

"You've left the desert," he said.

"Word travels fast," I said.

Clayton smiled. "I'm sorry for your marital failure."

"Sure," I said.

"Have you gotten to the bottom of this mess yet?" Blackstone's hands were motionless on the arms of my chair. His nails were buffed. He wore a large diamond on the ring finger of his right hand.

"Maybe it doesn't have a bottom," I said.

"Which means no, I take it," Blackstone said.

"Yeah," I said.

"Tell me what you know."

"Why?"

Garcia laughed, a short barking sound.

Blackstone shook his head without looking at him. He reached inside his suit jacket and came out with a pigskin leather wallet, the long kind that is too big to fit into your pants pocket. He took out five hundred-dollar bills and laid them one beside the other on the desk.

"That's why," he said.

"You wish to employ me?" I said.

Eddie laughed his harsh bark again. "See, Mr. Blackstone, I told you he was a smart guy."

Blackstone nodded.

"Yes," he said. "I wish to employ you. I want you to find out where my son-in-law is. I wish you to bring these two murder investigations to a satisfactory conclusion. I wish my daughter's life to be orderly and pleasant again."

"What if the orderly conclusion is that your son-in-law buttoned both of them?" I said.

Blackstone shrugged.

I looked at the five hundred. "I don't need this much retainer," I said.

"Take your usual retainer, keep the rest as advance against expenses."

I nodded. "Why me?" I said. "Why not buy a couple of cops or maybe a judge or a D.A. and have the whole thing called off?"

"My daughter wants her husband back," Blackstone said. "Your suggestion doesn't lead to that."

"Okay," I said. I leaned over and picked up the hundreds and put them in my wallet. There was nothing in there to crowd them.

"If you wish to reach me, call Eddie. He will put us in touch. He has my complete confidence." He leaned forward again and placed a small white card on my desk. It was blank, except that a phone number was written on it in black ink.

I looked at Eddie. "Mine too," I said.

"My only condition, Marlowe, is that you report everything to me. I am not employing you to gossip to the police."

"You get first look at everything," I said. "But there may be things that I'll have to report. I'm a licensed private investigator. There's only so far I can go for a client."

"As long as I'm first," Blackstone said. "We'll deal with any other eventualities as they arise."

"Dandy," I said.

He got up and turned. Eddie Garcia moved ahead of him and went out the door first. Blackstone followed. Neither of them said good-bye.

35

I was working again. Except for the fact there was money in my wallet I didn't feel much different than not working. I still didn't have any idea what to do to earn my retainer and advance against expenses. For a change of pace I swiveled my chair around and stared out the window at Hollywood Boulevard for a while. The first idea I had was that it was time to change the grease in the fryolator in the coffee shop downstairs. In the L.A. basin to the south, hard-looking thunderheads were building. The towers of downtown L.A. were in a grey overcast that stopped short of Hollywood. Here the sun still shone. But that was temporary. In a while the thunderheads would roll north and bump into the hills and the rain would come hard. I'd seen it before.

I watched the thunderheads move up toward me for a while, and then I swiveled around and got out one of the pictures of Muriel and slid it in a manila envelope. I put one of my cards in with it, and on the card I wrote, "Do you wish to tell me about this picture?" I put the Hollywood Boulevard address on the card, slipped the card in with the picture, sealed and addressed the envelope. Then I got up, went down to the post office and mailed it, special delivery, and went back to the office.

To pass time I bought myself the first drink from the new office bottle. I was finishing the next to last swallow and debating whether to have a second when I heard my outer door open again. Maybe I'd have to hire an assistant. I put the last swallow of bourbon down and got a confident smile on my face and in walked Les Valentine/Larry Victor.

"That was easy," I said.

"Huh?"

"Someone just hired me to find you," I said.

"Who?"

I shook my head.

"I called your office in Poodle Springs, and they said it was disconnected and so I called your wife, I hope you don't mind, and she said you were back here working."

I nodded. Larry looked like he'd been sleeping in bus terminals and washing in the men's room.

"Mind if I sit down?" he said.

I nodded toward the client chair. He sat, brushing his trousers as he did, as if he could put a crease back in them with his hands. He got seated and patted his breast pockets.

"Damn," he said, "I forgot to get some. You got a smoke?"

I slid the pack across the deck, a book of matches slipped inside between the package and the cellophane. He got one out and lit it and took in the smoke as if it were oxygen. He was wearing fawn-colored gabardine slacks and a yellow checked shirt buttoned to the neck and a cream-colored silk tweed sport coat with a pocket display handkerchief the color of a tequila sunrise. Or that's what everything had started out as. Now the clothes were rumpled and there were stains on the shirtfront. The show hankie had been used as a towel and was crumpled in the pocket of the coat so that only a scraggly end hung out. He hadn't shaved in several days and the beard that had emerged was patchy with a spattering of grey. The balding head looked mottled and he needed a haircut.

He saw me looking at him.

"Been on the go," he said. "Haven't gotten a chance to clean up today."

I nodded. The office bottle was still there. He was gazing at it the way a cow looks at a meadow.

"Want a drink?" I said.

"Sure could use one," he said. "Sun's over the yard-arm somewhere, right?"

I got up and got the other glass from the sink and brought it over and poured both of us a substantial drink. He grabbed his and guzzled nearly a third of it before he put the glass down on the edge of my desk. He didn't let go of it, just sat with the glass in his hand resting on the desktop. I got my pipe out and began to fill it. He drank another third of his drink, and when he put it down I picked up the bottle and refilled the glass. He looked like he was going to cry in gratitude. I got my pipe packed and fired, and took a small sip of the second drink.

"Nice set-up you got here," he said.

"For rats, maybe," I said. "Is there anything you came to see me about?"

"You're too hard on yourself. It's a nice office," he said. "Not showy, maybe, but that's all front anyway. You've seen my place. Serves fine. Desk, file cabinet, what the hell else do you need?"

He drank some more of the bourbon and leaned back as the booze relaxed him.

"Man, I'll tell you what, that came from the right barrel."

I waited. I knew he'd vamp around for a while, but I also knew he was desperate. He'd wanted me bad enough to call Linda. He leaned over and picked up my pack of cigarettes.

"Mind?" he said.

I shook my head. He lit up, dragged in some smoke, took a swig of bourbon, swallowed, let the smoke trail out.

"Cops still looking for me, I suppose," he said.

"Yes," I said. "Me too."

"I didn't kill that bimbo," he said. "Hell, you believe me, you helped me get away."

"That was mostly Angel," I said.

"Angel?"

"I told you, you looked happy together. I'm a sucker for happy together."

"Yeah, I guess maybe things ain't working out so well for you either," he said. "You moving back to town and all."

I puffed on my pipe.

"You don't think I killed her, do you?"

"I don't know anymore," I said. "How about Lippy?"

"Lippy?"

"Yeah, you kill him?"

"Lippy? Lippy's dead?"

"You didn't know?" I said.

"How would I know?" he said. "I haven't been to the Springs in a week or so."

"How'd you know he was killed in the last week?" I said.

"Jesus, I don't. I just heard about it and I figure it woulda been news in Poodle Springs."

"Un huh," I said.

"I didn't kill anybody, Marlowe. You're the only guy I can talk to, the only one I can level with."

"Like you did when I dropped you off at Muriel's. That you'd stay there where I could find you."

"Yeah, sure, I know. I know I ran out on you. But I had to. I had to get away from there. You don't know what she's like. Her money, her father, what she needs, what she wants, what I have to do . . . I was suffocating there, Marlowe."

I reached in my drawer and brought out one of the 8 × 10 glossy prints of Muriel Valentine. I held it up so he could see it.

"Tell me about this," I said.

"Jesus," he said. "Where did you get that?"

"It's the picture Lola Faithful showed you in the bar before she was killed, isn't it?" I said.

"Where'd you get it? Come on, Marlowe, where did you?"

"The tooth fairy," I said, "left it instead of a quarter."

He drank some more bourbon, stubbed out the cigarette in the round glass ashtray on my desk and took another one from the pack without asking.

"That's how I met her," he said.

"She was posing for dirty pictures?" I said.

"She liked it," he said. "People in the business knew about her. Ask anybody. Kinky rich girl, come in and get photographed in the nude. The thing is, the funny thing, is that she had to know the pictures would be used. She wanted them sold, you know, distributed. She wanted to know some guy on the street would pick her picture up from someplace and see it."

"So you proposed at once," I said.

"No, Jesus, Marlowe, you're a sarcastic bastard."

"I try," I said. "Did you take her right home to Angel and introduce her?"

"Damn it, it was my chance. I'd been nickel and diming it for years. Man, I'm a damn artist, and all I got to do to make a living was take dirty pictures. Here was this broad had more dough than Howard Hughes, right there, in my lap, all the dough I wanted; for me, sure, but for Angel. Kid deserves everything."

"And look what she got," I said.

"Marlowe," he said. "I don't know what to do. If the cops find me it's all going to come out."

"If you took her picture," I said, "how come she doesn't know you're Larry Victor?"

"I was using Valentine, then. You know, like a stage name. Had a studio on Highland, near Melrose. I was trying to do serious photography under my own name. And like when I got the chance to marry her, well, then I opened up a new office, under my real name."

"To keep Angel in the dark," I said.

"Yeah. I didn't want any connection with Les Valentine for Angel. She never knew I was using the name anyway."

"Your mother know who you are?" I said.

"Marlowe, I didn't kill anybody, but if the cops get me the whole thing's going to come out. Angel will know, Muriel will know."

"And her old man will know and he will send a very tough guy named Eddie Garcia around to ask you about how come you have made a big mess out of your marriage to his daughter."

I took one of the hundred-dollar bills that his father-in-law by bigamy had given me and handed it across the desk to Victor.

"There's a flophouse on Wilcox," I said. "Just south of the boulevard. The Starwalk Motel. Check in there, get cleaned up, have something to eat, and stay there. I'll do what I can. If you're not there when I want you, I tell everybody everything and you're on your own."

Victor took the bill and stared at it.

"What's your real name," I said. "Victor or Valentine?"

"Victor . . . well, originally it was Schlenker, but I had it changed."

"To Victor," I said. "Larry Victor."

He nodded.

"Okay, Larry. Go down there and wait for me."

"How long?" he said. "I mean, I need action. I can't hang out forever in some flop."

"Blackstone finds out and you'll be hanging out in the big flop in the sky," I said. "I'll do what I can."

Victor nodded too often and too rapidly. He got up and put my cigarettes in his shirt pocket and folded the hundred over once in his pants pocket.

"Leave the bottle," I said.

He smiled automatically and rubbed his chin with his open hand.

"I'll hear from you?" he said.

I nodded. He turned toward the door.

"I told Angel about Muriel," I said.

He stopped with his back to me.

"What'd she say?" he said without turning around.

"She didn't believe me," I said.

Still with his back to me, he said, "You tell Muriel?"

"No."

He nodded and without looking back went to the door, opened it and left.

36

I called Eddie Garcia at the number Blackstone had given me, and he agreed to meet me at the Bay City Pier. He was there when I got there, at the far end leaning on the rail watching the sea birds swoop over the waves looking for fish, and circle over the pier looking for garbage. The clouds had moved out of the basin now and the ocean was grey and sleek looking, the swells moving sluggishly under the overcast. A wind had moved in with the thunderheads and was whipping the tips of the swells and tearing a little spray loose from them. Garcia was wearing a light trench coat against the wind, the collar turned up.

As I approached Garcia he rolled around with his

back against the railing and his elbows resting on it and looked at me.

"Nice day you brought me out on, Sailor," he said.

"You picked the pier," I said.

"Good place to talk alone," he said.

I nodded. "Lot of open space so you can't be ambushed," I said.

In the daylight, up close, I could see the crows' feet around Garcia's eyes, the depth of the lines around his mouth. He didn't look tired, just older than I'd realized.

"So what'll it be, Sailor?"

"Tell me about Muriel Blackstone," I said.

Something seemed to move behind Garcia's eyes. His face remained blank.

"Why?" he said.

"I'm in a bind, Eddie," I said. "I can probably find Victor okay, and when I do I can see to it that he goes home to Muriel, but I don't know for sure that it's the best idea for anybody."

"Why not?" Garcia said.

"He's not a hell of a guy," I said.

Garcia barked his short laugh.

"We all know that," he said.

"There's other people involved," I said.

"I work for Blackstone," Garcia said. "So do you."

"Doesn't mean he owns me," I said. It didn't mean anything. I was just making noise, buying time, trying to figure out what I even wanted out of this.

"Doesn't mean he owns me either," Garcia said. "So what?"

"Does Blackstone know she's hinky?" I said.

Eddie straightened a little from his lounge on the railing. His eyes narrowed.

"Hinky," he said.

I had on a trench coat too; every well-dressed toughie had one. I reached inside it and brought out one of my pictures of Muriel. I felt like a man selling French postcards. Garcia took the picture and looked at it without expression. As he handed it back to me a raindrop splattered on it—one raindrop, a fat one, the size of a nickel. Around me on the pier I could hear other drops like that, spattering sporadically. I wiped the picture against my chest and slipped it back inside my coat.

Garcia looked at me with a faint smile. "Mr. Blackstone was here now you'd be dead," he said.

"He'd kill me?"

"He'd have me kill you," Eddie said.

"Yeah," I said. "I can feel my lips quivering."

"Where'd you get that photo?"

"Doesn't matter," I said. The rain was starting to

come harder, the nickel-sized drops coming more and more closely together. "Does Blackstone know about her?"

Garcia was silent, thinking. I stood and waited while he thought.

Finally he said, "Yeah. He knows. Kid's been wrong since she was little. Booze, creeps, dope. When she was younger I spent a lot of my time straightening out her life."

"Like what?" I said.

"Like she's shacking up with some Hollywood heartthrob up at Zuma Beach and I go up and have a talk with him and he leaves her alone. Like there was a magazine, nothing you ever heard of, the kind that puts out two issues and folds and opens up under another name. Anyway, they had a photo spread on her." Garcia grinned savagely. "*Blueblood Nymphet* it was going to be called. I went around and talked with the publisher. Like that."

"She met Victor when he took this photo," I said.

Garcia nodded. "Yeah. Blackstone took her to doctors, hell, we went over to Switzerland with her. Exhibitionism, they said. And a lot of other crap that don't mean anything to me. Didn't cure her, though, just talked a lot."

"You been with Blackstone a long time?" I said.

"Thirty-one years," Garcia said.

"That's more than just working for a man," I said.

"So where'd you get the picture, Sailor?" Garcia said. The rain was steady now, stippling the slick surface of the waves.

"Lola Faithful had it and stashed it in Union Station. I found the receipt in her house."

"How come the cops didn't find it?" Garcia said.

"They weren't looking for it," I said. "I saw the argument in the bar. I knew there was a picture."

"Where'd she get it?"

"I don't know," I said. "She was dead when I met her."

"And she tried to blackmail Larry with it," Garcia said.

I nodded. The rain had soaked Garcia's dark hair and water ran down his face. Garcia didn't seem to notice.

"And he capped her," he said.

I shrugged. "Maybe," I said. "Or maybe she went to others."

"Muffy?" Garcia said.

"Or maybe she went all the way, to the source," I said.

"Mr. Blackstone," Garcia said.

"Which probably means you. You use a small-caliber gun, hot-loaded?"

The top two buttons of Garcia's raincoat were un-buttoned. He made a movement and a gun appeared. He turned and fired, and a seagull spun out of mid-swoop and plummeted into the ocean. Garcia turned back and the gun was lying in his open palm. It was a squat .44 Magnum, nickel-plated with a two-inch bar-rel. It would have made a hole the size of a baseball in Lola Faithful's head. Garcia moved again and the gun was back inside his coat.

"Not bad," I said, "with that short a barrel."

"Keep it in mind," Garcia said. "I was you, I'd find myself Les Valentine, bring him back to Muffy, take Mr. Blackstone's dough and move on."

The heavy warm rain was hammering down on us like a bad headache. I could feel the wetness where it had seeped in around my collar. The wind had come with it now, hard, and pushed at both of us.

"Mr. Blackstone finally got her married, you under-stand? The guy's a creep, okay. You know it, I know it, Mr. Blackstone, he knows it. But Muffy don't know it, or if she does, she don't care. And Mr. Blackstone don't care either. He's got her under cover, out in the Springs, off the streets, safe. *Comprendez,* Sailor? You screw that up and Mr. Blackstone going to be sending me looking for you."

"If he does, Chico, you know where I am," I said.

And we stared at each other for a time in the rain, with the wind shoving at us and no one else in sight, out at the far end of the city pier above the fat grey ocean, a very long way from Poodle Springs.

37

It was suppertime when I got back from terrifying Eddie Garcia. I took a long shower and put on dry clothes and made myself a stiff Scotch and soda and sat down and called Linda. Tino answered.

"Mr. Marlowe," he said. "I am sorry you are away. I hope you will be back soon."

I murmured something encouraging, and waited while he got Linda. When she came on her voice was as clear as moonlight.

"Darling," she said. "Are you sheltered and warm?"

"I wanted you to have this phone number," I said, and gave it to her. "It's a furnished apartment on Ivar.

No houseboy, no pool, no piano bar. I don't know if I can survive."

"It is frightful, isn't it, how people choose to live," Linda said. "I hope at least you can get a civilized gimlet there."

"Sure," I said. "Anything you want, you can get in Hollywood, you know that."

"Are you lonely, darling?"

"Lonely, me? As soon as word got out that I was back in town there was a stampede of Paramount contract starlets up Western Ave."

We were both quiet for a moment on the telephone. The wires between us hummed faintly with tension.

"Darling, now don't be angry, but Daddy is opening a plant, something to do with ball bearings, in Long Beach and he suggested you might wish to consider a position there as, ah, director of security."

"No," I said.

"We could live in La Jolla, we own some property there, and you could drive to work in the morning and be home every evening by six-thirty."

"Can't be that way, Linda."

"I know," she said. "I knew it when I said it, but darling, I miss you so much. I miss you all the time and especially at night. I hate to sleep alone, darling."

"I miss you too," I said, "except when the starlets are here."

"You bastard," she said. "Why are you a bastard, why must you be so hard, why can't you bend a little?"

"It's all I have," I said. "I don't have money. I don't have prospects. All I have is who I am. All I have is a few private rules I've laid down for myself."

"I hear that, but damn it, I don't know what it means. All I know is that I love you, and I want you with me. Why is that so bad?"

"It isn't, it's good. But you want me to be different than I am. And if I change, I disappear. Because there isn't anything but what I am."

There was a long silence on the line and then Linda said softly, "Damn you, Marlowe, Goddamn you." She hung up softly and I held the receiver at my end for a moment and then put it gently back in the cradle.

I took a long pull at the Scotch and looked around the rented room at the rented furniture. It was as charming as Sears and Roebuck. I got up and walked to the window and looked out. It was dark. There was nothing to see but my own reflection in the black glass, streaked with rain: a 42-year-old man, drinking alone in a rented apartment in Hollywood while above the clouds the universe rolled slowly eastward over the dark plains of the Republic.

I turned away from the window and headed for the kitchen to refill my glass.

38

It was still raining the next morning, the kind of steady rain under solid clouds that makes you think it will never stop. I shook the water off my trench coat and hung it in the corner of my office. I had coffee in a paper cup that I had bought downstairs and, after my coat was put away, I sat down at my desk to sip it. I was wearing my .38 in a shoulder holster. Eddie Garcia had been talking pretty tough and, besides, if it kept raining I might have to shoot my way on board an ark.

The coffee was too hot for more than a shallow sip, and after one I put it on the corner of my desk where I could reach it when it cooled. My outer door opened and closed. There was a brief clack of heels and then

Muffy Blackstone came in out of the rain. She was wearing a scarlet raincoat and matching rain hat. Over her shoulder was a large black purse and her feet were protected by shiny black high-heeled boots. Her hands were plunged into the pockets of the coat. She took one of them out to close my inner door behind her, then she marched around in front of my desk and stared down at me.

"Good weather for ducks," I said pleasantly.

She kept staring. I nodded at the coffee on the corner of my desk. A small tassel of steam drifted up from it.

"Care for a sip?" I said. "I don't have another cup, but I brushed my teeth good this morning."

She took her hands out of her pockets and opened her big shoulder purse and took out the manila envelope I'd mailed her.

She tossed it on my desk without a word. I reached out, took it, took the picture out. I looked at the picture and then carefully at her, turning my head sideways at one point to compare her face with that in the picture.

"Yep," I said finally, "that's you."

"Where did you get it?" she said. Her face was very tight but her voice was surprisingly lilting.

"Lola Faithful had it hidden," I said. "I found it in the checked-baggage room at Union Station."

"Why did you send it to me?" she said. The lilt in

her voice was more pronounced. It wasn't calmness, I realized, it was the sing-song of hysteria.

"I have been walking around the edges of this case since I started. I thought maybe if I couldn't get in I could get someone to come out."

"You are . . . trying . . ." Her voice began to go on her. It would rise in a fluty way and then fail and she'd start again in the lower registers. "You . . . are trying . . . to ruin . . . my marriage," she trilled.

I shook my head. "No, I'm trying to find your husband, and I'm trying to find out who killed Lola Faithful and Lippy," I said. "And so far I'm not doing a hell of a job at it."

"Who . . . To whom have you . . . shown this . . . picture?"

"I have not shown it to your father," I said.

"You leave my father out of this, you filthy . . ." The words came in a rush and she had no finish for them. She couldn't think of anything filthy enough to fit me.

"I thought you liked having your picture passed around," I said. "How come you're throwing a wingding?"

"What do you know?" she said, and her voice was no longer lilting. It had sunk into her chest. There was a little bubble of saliva at the left corner of her mouth. She was still standing in front of the desk, her feet wide apart, her hands back in the pockets of her raincoat. She wore bright red lipstick and a lot of stuff on her eyes, but her face was pale, nearly chalky, as if she'd never seen the desert.

"I know you met Les when he was taking pictures out of an office down on Highland Ave. I know you liked posing nude, liked having the picture distributed, wanted it to be seen. I know you've had a life full of dope and booze and a string of wrong guys, and I know your old man has bailed you out of every one."

"Or sent Eddie," she said. The bubble of saliva was still there.

I waited. She gnawed a little on her lower lip, enough to smear the thick lipstick. She licked the corners of her mouth with the tip of her tongue. First the right, then the left. The saliva bubble disappeared.

"You working for my father?" she said.

"He hired me to find Larry for you, and bring him back."

"Don't call him that," she said, her voice still in her chest. "Don't call him Larry."

"Sure," I said.

"He doesn't want you to bring him back to me. He just wants you to find him so Eddie can kill him."

"Why would he do that?" I said.

"Because he won't let anyone have me. He'll never let me go. He finds a way, always."

"How come he let you marry Les?" I said.

"We ran away and when we came back we were already married," she said. "It was too late."

"That wouldn't have bothered a guy like Blackstone," I said. "A little thing like marriage? And it sure wouldn't bother Eddie Garcia."

"I knew you wouldn't believe me," she said. Her voice was starting to flute upward again. "No one will. He'll ruin this too . . . like he ruined everything . . . and you'll help him."

The saliva had appeared again at the corner of her mouth, and her voice was into the range where only dogs could hear her. "Why don't you sit down, Mrs. Valentine," I said. Her hands came out of her pockets again, and in her right hand was a gun. It wasn't very big. It was silver plated and what I could see of the handle was pearl. It was a cute gun, a gun for a lady to carry, a nice little cute automatic, probably a .25. Maybe hot-loaded. The cruel black eye of the gun never wavered as she pointed it at me. It wouldn't make a very big hole in my forehead. Probably wouldn't even make an exit wound, just ricochet around inside there so the coroner could find it with no trouble when they did the autopsy on me downtown.

She held the gun in both hands, straight out in front of her, her knees bent a little, feet comfortably apart just like someone taught her. Her mouth was open and her tongue moved rapidly back and forth across her lower lip. She was breathing through her nose in little snorts.

"He loves me," she said. "And I won't . . . let . . . you . . . spoil . . ."

Everything moved very slowly. The rain uncoiled with infinite leisure against the window behind me. I could see a stray drop of rainwater meander down the lapel of Muriel's raincoat.

"They've all been trying to spoil it," I said. "Haven't they?"

"Yes," she whispered.

"And you had to kill them?"

"Yes," again a whisper, the word drawn out into a long hiss.

"Lola," I said. She nodded slowly. "Lippy." Again the nod.

I reached forward slowly and picked up my coffee. "But not me," I said. "I'm trying to help. I know where Larry is."

She shook her head slowly. Everything was very slow.

"You . . . won't . . . spoil . . . it," she said.

I dropped my coffee cup. The coffee sloshed out on my pants leg as the cup bounced on my thigh and went to the floor.

"Oops," I said and bent to pick it up and went out of the chair behind my desk digging the .38 out from under my arm as I went. I hit the floor on my left shoulder. Above me there was a flat snap and then another and two bullets buried in the wall behind my desk chair. I fired one shot straight up to the ceiling, to let her know I had a gun. I had rolled onto my knees now, still down behind the desk, and I waited with the .38 poised at the edge of the desktop. I could hear her fast shallow breathing.

"I don't want to shoot you," I said and edged around the corner of the desk low. I heard her heels, then the door. I stood and saw my outer office door swing shut. I walked to the window and looked down at Hollywood Boulevard. In maybe a minute I saw her come out into the wet street and turn right and head up Hollywood, walking fast with her head down and her hands still in her raincoat pockets.

Most of the cars on the boulevard had their headlights on in the slate-grey morning. They shone on the wet pavement and blended with the colored neon reflections and the sheen of the roofs of wet cars as I watched her until out of sight, moving west toward the Chinese Theater, past the souvenir shops and the places that sold peekaboo underwear.

I turned away and took the empty shell out of the cylinder and put in a fresh one and stored the gun back under my arm. I got some paper towels and cleaned up the spilled coffee and threw the paper cup away. I looked at the bullet holes in the wall and the one in the ceiling. Nothing much I could do about those. Probably just as well to leave them. Be good for my image. I got my trench coat back on and headed out to get my car out of the lot up Cahuenga.

I was in no hurry. I was pretty sure where she'd go. There wasn't anyplace else.

39

I sometimes think that Southern California looks better in the rain than any other time. The rain washes away the dust and glazes the cheapness and poverty and pretense, and freshens the trees and flowers and grass that the sun has blasted. Bel Air under the wet sky was all emerald and scarlet and gold with the rain making the streets glisten.

I told the guy at Clayton Blackstone's gate, "Marlowe. I'm working for Mr. Blackstone."

The guard went back inside the shack. Only in Bel Air would it be a shack. In Thousand Oaks it would have been a two-bedroom ranch with a garden. After two or three minutes the guard came out and said, "Wait here, Eddie'll be down to get you."

I sat and watched the wipers make their truncated triangle on my windshield. In another maybe three minutes a car pulled up inside the gate, Eddie Garcia got out, the gate opened and Eddie walked over to my car with the collar of his trench coat turned up. He got in beside me.

"Follow the other car," he said.

We went up the winding driveway with the wet greenery around us and pulled in under the big front entrance. The car ahead stopped and J.D. got out and stared back at me. Garcia got out his side and I got out on mine. Garcia jerked his head and I followed him into the office and he led me through the library to Blackstone's office. Neither one of us said a word.

Blackstone was behind the big desk again, this time wearing a double-breasted blue blazer and white tennis shirt. There was some kind of crest on the breast pocket of the blazer. Standing near the bar, with a drink in her hand, where I had expected her to be, was Muriel. Her cute gun was not in sight. Eddie closed the door behind us when we came into the room and stood a foot or so inside the door, with his back to it. I walked across and took the same chair near Blackstone's desk that I'd sat in before.

"Raining," Blackstone said absently.

"Even in Bel Air," I said.

He nodded, staring past me at his daughter.

"You were pretty straight with me, Marlowe, last time you were here."

I waited.

"But you kept some things back," he said.

"Never said I didn't."

He spoke slowly and almost without inflection. Like a man thinking of other things: lost romances, children playing on a beach, things like that. He leaned forward and got a cigar from a box and trimmed it carefully with a knife he took from the middle drawer of the desk. He lit it carefully, turning the end slowly in the flame, and then took a puff, let the smoke out and watched it disperse in the air-conditioned atmosphere. Nobody spoke while this went on. Through the picture window I could see the rain dimpling the surface of the cerulean water in the pool.

"Now, Marlowe, what have you to tell me?"

"Your daughter stopped by my office," I said. "Just before she came here."

"Oh?" He looked at Muriel. Muriel held on to the glass in both hands. It was nearly full; she seemed to have forgotten about drinking from it.

"What was the substance of your discussion?" he said.

"That you were intent on destroying her marriage and I, as your agent, was being employed to the same end."

Blackstone stared at his daughter. "Muriel?"

She didn't answer. She was holding her glass against her breast, as if trying to warm the drink.

"She said she would kill me as she had Lola and Lippy," I said, "and then she pulled a .25 automatic with a chrome finish and pearl handle grips and began plugging away."

Blackstone didn't change expressions or move. He gazed at me like a man lost in contemplation.

"Lippy and Lola were shot with a .25," I said.

Blackstone nodded slowly, but he wasn't looking at me. He was gazing across the room at his daughter. He stood, finally. I could see that he was wearing white slacks and white loafers. He walked across the room and stood maybe three feet in front of his daughter.

"There is nothing, Muffy, that I cannot buy or frighten. Nothing so broken that I cannot fix it."

She didn't look at him.

"Tell me about this," Blackstone said. "About the gun and Lola and Lippy. Tell me about what Mr. Marlowe has said."

"Lola had a bad picture of me," Muriel said; her voice was childish. "The kind I used to pose for a long time ago."

Blackstone nodded. "You're not doing that anymore, are you, Muffy?" he said.

She shook her head, still staring at the floor, her glass still clutched to her chest.

"She said she would show it to all the people at the Springs and tell people that Les took it, and . . ." She shook her head without looking up.

"And?" Blackstone said.

Muriel didn't move.

"And she arranged to meet Lola at Larry's office and when she got the picture she shot her," I said. "And took the picture and cleaned out Larry's files and left."

"Didn't she know there'd be other pictures?" Blackstone said.

"She's not playing with all the dots on her dice," I said. "She didn't know that it would implicate Larry and lead people to Les either."

We were talking about her as if she were a jade ornament.

"What about Lippy?" he said to Muriel. "I didn't even know you knew him."

"He hired Mr. Marlowe to find Les, to harass him over money. He owed Mr. Lipshultz money."

Blackstone looked at me once, hard. I shrugged.

"Did you know that Mr. Lipshultz worked for me, Muffy?"

"Not until Mr. Marlowe said."

"Even so, why didn't you just come to me? I could have given you money. I've done it before."

She stared at the floor.

"Why, Muffy?"

"I was ashamed," she said. "I didn't want you to know Les was in debt from gambling. So I went out to talk with Mr. Lipshultz."

"Did Lippy know your daughter?" I said.

"No. He didn't know I had one. I kept business very separate from family." He turned back to his daughter. "What happened, Muffy?"

"I asked him not to bother Les and me, and he said business was business and his boss would nail his hide to the club door if he lost an IOU for that much. And I said I didn't have the money but there were other ways I could pay."

"Jesus," Blackstone said softly.

His daughter didn't speak.

"And so Lippy gets a smile like Br'er Bear," I said, "and he tells the shooters to hit the road and pours out a Scotch and says, 'How do you like the view of the desert here, sweetie,' and . . ." I shot an imaginary gun, dropping my thumb on my extended forefinger.

"He would have . . . ruined . . . it," Muriel said. I'd heard that sound before.

Blackstone stood and looked down at his daughter for a long moment. Then he turned and walked back behind his desk and sank into the chair. He picked up his cigar and puffed on it to see that it was still going and leaned back and stared silently across the room at his daughter. But when he spoke it was to me.

"I had Eddie chase Larry Victor down," he said. "See what was cooking." He paused, looking at his cigar. "You know he's got a wife."

"Yeah," I said. "I've known it all along."

"And didn't see any need to tell me that even when you took my five hundred dollars."

"Until I had the lay of it," I said, "I thought it would only hurt."

"What are you saying?" Muriel said. "What . . . are . . . you . . . talking about?"

"He had another wife, Muffy," Blackstone said. "The guy you killed two people for had another wife."

"What . . . do . . . you . . . mean . . . another . . . wife?"

"He's married to another woman at the same time

he's married to you, Muffy," Blackstone said. "He's a bigamist."

The silence in the room imploded, getting denser and denser like a collapsing star. Against the door Eddie Garcia looked as if he might be asleep, except that his eyes moved languidly from time to time.

"That's . . . not . . . true," Muriel said in her lilting whisper. "It's not . . . true."

Blackstone was looking at me now.

"Where do you stand, Marlowe?"

"She killed two people," I said. "I can't lindy off into the sunset on that."

"And I can't let her go down for it," he said.

Muriel straightened at the bar and half turned and, using both hands, put the drink down carefully on the bar.

"I won't stand here and listen to lies," she said. Her voice was in its lower register.

Blackstone shook his head. "No, Muffy," he said. "You're too shaky now, you need to calm down for a while."

"You sit there and make up lies," she said. Her voice was still deep but her breath was coming short and she spoke in basso profundo gasps. "You want to . . . ruin my marriage." She was moving slowly across the room, her hands back in her pockets. Eddie stood in the doorway as if he were observing the Big Dipper. "You won't let anyone . . . have me. Never. You . . . ruin it."

"Muffy," Blackstone said. There was more sharpness in his voice.

She turned suddenly. Her hands came out of her pockets, the gun in her right. She clasped her left hand over the right and dropped into her shooter's stance and put two bullets into Blackstone's forehead. I was half turned in my seat when the side of her head spurted blood and the heavy thump of Garcia's big magnum sounded and Muriel spun halfway round and fell facedown on the floor.

I checked both of them in the resonant silence that followed the gunfire, smelling the cordite in the room. They were both dead. Garcia was still holding his gun, standing by the door. "Half a second," he said. "I was half a second late."

I nodded.

"Ten years ago," Garcia said softly. "Ten years ago I could have saved him."

"Cops will pour it on you, Eddie, if they make you for this," I said.

"They won't find me, Marlowe."

"Still pretty fair shooting," I said. "She had the jump."

"Half second," Garcia said again, "half second slow." Then he opened the door and closed it and was gone.

I went slowly to Blackstone's desk and picked up the phone and dialed a number I knew a lot better than I wanted to.

40

The cops turned me loose in the middle of the afternoon. They didn't want to, but there was nothing to hold me for, except being a lousy detective, and they had their own problems with that. As I drove down the coast highway toward Venice I tried to sort out how bad a detective I'd been. By the time I reached Santa Monica I had decided I couldn't sort it out and might as well think I'd been a good detective for all the difference it made.

I parked behind the restaurant where Angel worked and went and said, "Tell the boss there's an emergency, and come with me."

Her eyes widened, but she didn't ask questions.

In five minutes we were in my Olds heading for Hollywood.

"There's no emergency," I said in the car. "I made that up to get you away."

"Have you found Larry?"

"Yeah, I have," I said. "I'm taking you to him."

"Oh my God," she said. "Is he all right?"

"Sure," I said. Though I wasn't sure Larry Victor would ever be all right.

We drove in silence then. The rain had tapered to a drizzle, just enough to engage the wipers.

"About being married to another woman," I said.

"I know that's not true," she said.

"Yeah, that's right," I said. "I was wrong about that."

By the time we pulled up in front of the motel where Larry was stashed the rain had stopped altogether.

The motel was one of those two-story affairs with each door painted a different color and a balcony running across the second floor. There were stairs at each end of the balcony. The office at the far end jutted out at right angles and was faced with some sort of artificial stone.

Angel and I went up the stairs to Victor's room. I knocked on the door.

"It's Marlowe," I said.

And in a moment I heard footsteps and then the door opened about three inches and Victor peeked out. I stepped aside and he saw Angel.

"Larry," she said. "Larry, it's me."

He closed the door, took the chain off and opened it again, and Angel seemed to elevate into his arms.

"Larry," she said. "Oh my God, Larry."

I leaned against the wall outside the door for a few minutes and smoked a cigarette and looked at the movement of the rain clouds as they began to break up. Then I went into the room. Angel and Larry were sitting on the bed holding hands. She was looking at him as if he were King of all the Persians.

I said, "Muriel Blackstone is dead. So is her father. Being who he was there's going to be a mess. How you handle it is your problem."

"How?" Victor said. "Who?"

"Doesn't matter," I said. "Wasn't you, and it wasn't me."

"That's the woman you said Larry was married to," Angel said.

"I was deceived by appearances," I said.

"Yeah, that's right," Victor said. "Appearances will deceive you sometimes."

"I don't know you're here," I said. "I don't know where you are."

I took the remaining four hundreds that Blackstone had given me out of my wallet and laid them on the cheap desk by the door.

"Don't call me up," I said. "Don't come see me."

I turned and went out the door. Victor followed me.

"Wait a minute," he said and came out on the balcony. "What if the cops come?"

"They will," I said. "If they can find you."

"But what should I do?"

"Stay away from me," I said. "And take care of that girl. If I ever hear you weren't good to her, I will track you down and stomp on your face."

"Hey, Marlowe, no need to talk like that. Hell, we've been through a lot together."

"Yeah," I said. "Remember what I told you."

I turned and went. Behind me I heard Victor say, "Marlowe? For chrissake, Marlowe."

I kept going.

I heard Angel say, "Good-bye, Mr. Marlowe. Thank you."

I waved without looking back. Then I was in my car and out on Wilcox Ave.

41

It was too late to go back to the office and too early to go back to my furnished apartment and count the walls. Maybe later. I'd set up a chess problem, have a couple of drinks, smoke my pipe. But not yet. If I started now the evening would be too long.

So I cruised slowly around Hollywood looking at the hustlers and pimps, the tourists and hookers, the people from Plainfield, New Jersey, looking for stars, the prom queens from Shakopee, Minnesota, veterans already of the casting couches. They were all there on the boulevard, frightened, eager, angry, desperate, just and unjust, mingling, hurrying, hanging around, trying to get ahead, get a stake, get a chance, a kind word;

looking for money, for love, for a place to sleep, trying to score some dope, some booze, something to eat; most of them alone, almost all of them lonely.

I found a spot to park across the street and got out and went into the bar at the Roosevelt. I had a double vodka gimlet and sat at the end of the bar to drink it. The after-office crowd was beginning to drift in. I looked at the bar light coming through the nearly straw-colored gimlet. It had been a long time since I'd sat in this bar and had a gimlet with Terry Lennox, a long time since I'd first met Linda Loring. Harlan Potter's daughter: gold and diamonds and silk, and perfume that cost more than my weekly wage. A long time, and I was still at the end of the bar when it was over, drinking alone.

Too bad, Marlowe. Too bad there wasn't any other way.

I drank the rest of my gimlet and got up and went out, and drove home.

My apartment had the musty, closed-up smell that they get when nothing human is in them all day. I left the hall door open and went and threw up a couple of windows in the living room to let the air blow through. The clouds were broken now and off to the west colored with the sun as it began to set. I left the windows and door open and went to the kitchen to make a drink. I put ice and soda in a glass with a shot of Scotch and carried it back to the living room. Linda was there. She had come in and closed the door. Beside her on the floor was a small overnight case. She wore a little pink suit and a silly pink hat the size of a throw rug and white gloves and shoes. Her overnight case was pink with white trim and had her initials on it. L.M.

"In town for long?" I said.

She didn't answer, only looked at me, and her eyes were enormous and simultaneously dark and luminous.

"This is a community property state," I said. "Did you come to carry off half my ammunition?"

"I came to make love with you," she said.

"I thought we were getting divorced," I said.

"Yes," she said, "we are. But it doesn't cover making love."

"You seem awfully sure of yourself," I said. "Overnight case and all. What if I said no?"

Linda smiled and shook her head. I felt as if I might disappear into her eyes if I looked at them too long.

"You're right," I said. "I probably won't say no."

She smiled a little wider, still silent, still with eternity lurking behind her eyes. She reached up and unpinned the silly pink hat and put it on the coffee table.

"I need to know what all this means to us," I said.

She nodded slowly.

"It means," she said, and her voice was almost detached, as if in tune with an orchestra playing out of earshot, "that we love each other too much to give each other up. We can end the marriage, but we cannot end the love. Probably we can't live together. But why must that mean we can't be lovers?"

"Oh," I said, "I see. That's what it means."

"Yes."

"Well, it makes sense to me," I said.

Linda unbuttoned the suit jacket and took it off, and unzipped her skirt and slid out of it. She took off her undergarments and let them drop to the floor and stood up straight and smiled at me some more.

"Do you wish to have me ravage you here on the living room floor or would you prefer to retire to the bedroom?" I said. I seemed disconnected now from my voice, as well, as if reality were off camera and we were enacting a poem that someone else had chanted. Linda didn't answer.

"What's your preference?" I heard myself say.

"I think both," I heard Linda say. And later, much later in the darkness, with the world put far aside, I heard one of us say, "forever?" and the other, I don't know which, our voices had merged by then, answered, "forever."

THE END